MEDITERRANEAN DOCTORS

*Demanding, devoted and
drop-dead gorgeous—these Latin doctors
will make your heart race!*

Smolderingly sexy Mediterranean doctors

Saving lives by day…red-hot lovers by night

Read these four MEDITERRANEAN
DOCTORS stories in this new collection
by your favorite authors, available from
Harlequin Presents EXTRA October 2008:

The Sicilian Doctor's Mistress
Sarah Morgan

The Italian Count's Baby
Amy Andrews

Spanish Doctor, Pregnant Nurse
Carol Marinelli

The Spanish Doctor's Love-Child
Kate Hardy

SARAH MORGAN was born in Wiltshire and started writing at the age of eight, when she produced an autobiography of her hamster.

At the age of eighteen she traveled to London to train as a nurse in one of London's top teaching hospitals, and she describes those years as extremely happy and definitely censored!

She worked in a number of areas after she qualified, but her favorite was A&E, where she found the work stimulating and fun. Nowhere else in the hospital environment did she encounter such good teamwork between doctors and nurses.

By now her interests had moved on from hamsters to men, and she started writing romance fiction.

Her first completed manuscript, written after the birth of her first child, was rejected but the comments were encouraging, so she tried again. On the third attempt, her manuscript *Worth the Risk* was accepted unchanged. She describes receiving the acceptance letter as one of the best moments of her life, after meeting her husband and having her two children.

Sarah still works part-time in a health-related industry, and spends the rest of the time with her family, trying to squeeze in writing whenever she can. She is an enthusiastic skier and walker, and loves outdoor life.

THE SICILIAN DOCTOR'S MISTRESS

SARAH MORGAN

~ MEDITERRANEAN DOCTORS ~

HARLEQUIN®

TORONTO • NEW YORK • LONDON
AMSTERDAM • PARIS • SYDNEY • HAMBURG
STOCKHOLM • ATHENS • TOKYO • MILAN • MADRID
PRAGUE • WARSAW • BUDAPEST • AUCKLAND

ISBN-13: 978-0-373-82371-0
ISBN-10:   0-373-82371-1

THE SICILIAN DOCTOR'S MISTRESS

First North American Publication 2008.

Previously published in the U.K. under the title
THE SICILIAN DOCTOR'S PROPOSAL.

www.eHarlequin.com

Printed in U.S.A.

THE SICILIAN
DOCTOR'S MISTRESS

PROLOGUE

'I DON'T believe in love. And neither do you.' Alice put her pen down and stared in bemusement at her colleague of five years. Had he gone mad?

'That was before I met Trish.' His expression was soft and far-away, his smile bordering on the idiotic. 'It's finally happened. Just like the fairy-tales.'

She wanted to ask if he'd been drinking, but didn't want to offend him. 'This isn't like you at all, David. You're an intelligent, hard-working doctor and at the moment you're talking like a—like a...' *A seven-year-old girl?* No, she couldn't possibly say that. 'You're not sounding like yourself,' she finished lamely.

'I don't care. She's the one. And I have to be with her. Nothing else matters.'

'Nothing else matters?' On the desk next to her the phone suddenly rang, but for once Alice ignored it. 'It's the start of the summer season, the village is already filling with tourists, most of the locals are struck down by that horrid virus, you're telling me you're leaving and you don't think it matters? Please, tell me this is a joke, David, please tell me that.'

Even with David working alongside her she was

working flat out to cope with the demand for medical care at the moment. It wasn't that she didn't like hard work. Work was her life. *Work had saved her.* But she knew her limits.

David dragged both hands through his already untidy hair. 'Not leaving exactly, Alice. I just need the summer off. To be with Trish. We need to decide on our future. We're in love!'

Love. Alice stifled a sigh of exasperation. Behind every stupid action was a relationship, she mused silently. She should know that by now. She'd seen it often enough. Why should David be different? Just because he'd *appeared* to be a sane, rational human being—

'You'll hate London.'

'Actually, I find London unbelievably exciting,' David confessed. 'I love the craziness of it all, the crowds of people all intent on getting somewhere yesterday, no one interested in the person next to them—' He broke off with an apologetic wave of his hand. 'I'm getting carried away. But don't you ever feel trapped here, Alice? Don't you ever wish you could do something in this village without the whole place knowing?'

Alice sat back in her chair and studied him carefully. She'd never known David so emotional. 'No,' she said quietly. 'I like knowing people and I like people knowing me. It helps when it comes to understanding their medical needs. They're our responsibility and I take that seriously.'

It was what had drawn her to the little fishing village in the first place. And now it felt like home. And the people felt like family. *More than her own ever had.* Here, she fitted. She'd found her place and she couldn't imagine living anywhere else. She loved the narrow cobbled streets, the busy harbour, the tiny shops selling shells and the trendy store selling surfboards and wet-suits. She loved the summer when the streets were crowded with tourists and she loved the winter when the beaches were empty and lashed by rain. For a moment she thought of London with its muggy, traffic-clogged streets and then she thought of her beautiful house. The house overlooking the broad sweep of the sea. The house she'd lovingly restored in every spare moment she'd had over the past five years.

It had given her sanctuary and a life that suited her. A life that was under her control.

'Since we're being honest here…' David took a deep breath and straightened, his eyes slightly wary. 'I think you should consider leaving, too. You're an attractive, intelligent woman but you're never going to find someone special buried in a place like this. You never meet anyone remotely eligible. All you think about is work, work and work.'

'David, I don't want to meet anyone.' She spoke slowly and clearly so that there could be no misunder-standing. 'I love my life the way it is.'

'Work shouldn't be your life, Alice. You need love.' David stopped pacing and placed a hand on his chest. 'Everyone needs love.'

Something inside her snapped. 'Love is a word used to justify impulsive, irrational and emotional behav-iour,' she said tartly, 'and I prefer to take a logical, sci-entific approach to life.'

David looked a little shocked. 'So, you're basically saying that I'm impulsive, irrational and emotional?'

She sighed. It was unlike her to be so honest. *To reveal so much about herself.* And unlike her to risk hurting someone's feelings. On the other hand, he was behaving very oddly. 'You're giving up a great job on the basis of a feeling that is indefinable, notoriously unpredictable and invariably short-lived so yes, I suppose I am saying that.' She nibbled her lip. 'It's the truth, so you can hardly be offended. You've said it yourself often enough.'

'That was before I met Trish and discovered how wrong I was.' He shook his head and gave a wry smile. 'You just haven't met the right person. When you do, everything will make sense.'

'Everything already makes perfect sense, thank you.' She reached for a piece of paper and a pen. 'If I draft an advert now, I just might find a locum for August.'

If she was lucky.

And if she wasn't lucky, she was in for a busy summer, she thought, her logical brain already involved in making lists. The village with its pretty harbour and quaint shops might not attract the medical profession but it attracted tourists by the busload and her work increased accordingly, especially during the summer months.

David frowned. 'Locum?' His brow cleared. 'You don't need to worry about a locum. I've sorted that out.'

Her pen stilled. 'You've sorted it out?'

'Of course.' He rummaged in his pocket and pulled out several crumpled sheets of paper. 'Did you really think I'd leave you without arranging a replacement?'

Yes, she'd thought exactly that. All the people she'd ever known who'd claimed to be 'in love' had immediately ceased to give any thought or show any care to those around them.

'Who?'

'I have a friend who is eager to work in England. His qualifications are fantastic—he trained as a plastic surgeon but had to switch because he had an accident. Tragedy, actually.' David frowned slightly. 'He was brilliant, by all accounts.'

A plastic surgeon?

Alice reached for the papers and scanned the CV. 'Giovanni Moretti.' She looked up. 'He's Italian?'

'Sicilian.' David grinned. 'Never accuse him of being Italian. He's very proud of his heritage.'

'This man is well qualified.' She put the papers down on her desk. 'Why would he want to come here?'

'You want to work here,' David pointed out logically, 'so perhaps you're just about to meet your soulmate.' He caught her reproving look and shrugged. 'Just joking. Everyone is entitled to a change of pace. He was working in Milan, which might explain it but, to be honest, I don't really know why he wants to come here. You know us men. We don't delve into details.'

Alice sighed and glanced at the CV on her desk. He'd probably only last five minutes, but at least he might fill the gap while she looked for someone to cover the rest of the summer.

'Well, at least you've sorted out a replacement. Thanks for that. And what happens at the end of the summer? Are you coming back?'

David hesitated. 'Can we see how it goes? Trish and I have some big decisions to make.' His eyes gleamed at the prospect. 'But I promise not to leave you in the lurch.'

He looked so happy, Alice couldn't help but smile. 'I wish you luck.'

'But you don't understand, do you?'

She shrugged. 'If you ask me, the ability to be ruled by emotion is the only serious flaw in the human make-up.'

'Oh, for goodness' sake.' Unexpectedly, David reached out and dragged her to her feet. 'It's out there, Alice. Love. You just have to look for it.'

'Why would I want to? If you want my honest opinion, I'd say that love is just a temporary psychiatric condition that passes given sufficient time. Hence the high divorce rate.' She pulled her hands away from his, aware that he was gaping at her.

'*A temporary psychiatric condition?*' He gave a choked laugh and his hands fell to his sides. 'Oh, Alice, you *have* to be joking. That can't really be what you believe.'

Alice tilted her head to one side and mentally reviewed all the people she knew who'd behaved oddly in the name of love. There were all too many of them. Her parents and her sister included. 'Yes, actually.' Her tone was flat as she struggled with feelings that she'd managed to suppress for years. Feeling suddenly agitated, she picked up a medical journal and scanned the contents, trying to focus her mind on fact. Facts were safe and comfortable. Emotions were dangerous and uncomfortable. 'It's exactly what I believe.'

Her heart started to beat faster and she gripped the journal more tightly and reminded herself that her life was under her control now. She was no longer a child at the mercy of other people's emotional transgressions.

David watched her. 'So you still don't believe love exists? Even seeing how happy I am?'

She turned. 'If you're talking about some fuzzy, indefinable emotion that links two people together then, no, I don't think that exists. I don't believe in the existence of an indefinable emotional bond any more than I believe in Father Christmas and the tooth fairy.'

David shook his head in disbelief. 'But I *do* feel a powerful emotion.'

She couldn't bring herself to put a dent in his happiness by saying more, so she stepped towards him and took his face in her hands. 'I'm pleased for you. Really I am.' She reached up and kissed him on the cheek. 'But it isn't "love". She sat back down and David studied her with a knowing, slightly superior smile on his face.

'It's going to happen to you, Alice.' He folded his arms across his chest and his tone rang with conviction. 'One of these days you're going to be swept off your feet.'

'I'm a scientist,' she reminded him, amusement sparkling in her blue eyes as they met the challenge in his. 'I have a logical brain. I don't believe in being swept off my feet.'

He stared at her for a long moment. 'No. Which is why it's likely to happen. Love strikes when you're not looking for it.'

'That's measles,' Alice said dryly, reaching for a pile of results that needed her attention. 'Talking of which, little Fiona Ellis has been terribly poorly since her bout of measles last winter. I'm going to check up on her today. See if there's anything else we can do. And I'm going to speak to Gina, the health visitor, about our MMR rates.'

'They dipped slightly after the last newspaper scare but I thought they were up again. The hospital has been keeping an eye on Fiona's hearing,' David observed, and Alice nodded.

'Yes, and I gather there's been some improvement. All the same, the family need support and we need to make sure that no one else in our practice suffers unnecessarily.' She rose to her feet and smiled at her partner. 'And that's what we give in a small community. Support and individual care. Don't you think you'll miss that? In London you'll end up working in one of those huge health centres with thousands of doctors and you probably won't get to see the same patient twice. You won't know them and they won't know you. It will be completely impersonal. Like seeing medical cases on a production line.'

She knew all the arguments, of course. She understood that a large group of GPs working together could afford a wider variety of services for their patients—psychologists, chiropodists—but she still believed that a good family doctor who knew his patients intimately was able to provide a superior level of care.

'You'll like Gio,' David said, strolling towards the door. 'Women always do.'

'As long as he does his job,' Alice said crisply, 'I'll like him.'

'He's generally considered a heartthrob.' There was a speculative look on his face as he glanced towards her. 'Women go weak at the knees when he walks into a room.'

Great. The last thing she needed was a Romeo who was distracted by everything female.

'Some women are foolish like that.' Alice stood up and reached for her jacket. 'Just as long as he doesn't break more hearts than he heals, then I really don't mind what he does when he isn't working here.'

'There's more to life than work, Alice.'

'Then go out there and enjoy it,' she advised, a smile on her face. 'And leave me to enjoy mine.'

CHAPTER ONE

GIOVANNI MORETTI stood at the top of the narrow cobbled street, flexed his broad shoulders to try and ease the tension from the journey and breathed in the fresh, clean sea air. Above him, seagulls shrieked and swooped in the hope of benefiting from the early morning catch.

Sounds of the sea.

He paused for a moment, his fingers tucked into the pockets of his faded jeans, his dark eyes slightly narrowed as he scanned the pretty painted cottages that led down to the busy harbour. Window-boxes and terracotta pots were crammed full with brightly coloured geraniums and tumbling lobelia and a smile touched his handsome face. Before today he'd thought that places like this existed only in the imagination of artists. It was as far from the dusty, traffic-clogged streets of Milan as it was possible to be, and he felt a welcome feeling of calm wash over him.

He'd been right to agree to take this job, he mused silently, remembering all the arguments he'd been presented with. Right to choose this moment to slow the pace of his life and leave Italy.

It was early in the morning but warm, tempting smells of baking flavoured the air and already the street seemed alive with activity.

A few people in flip-flops and shorts, who he took to be tourists, meandered down towards the harbour in search of early morning entertainment while others jostled each other in their eagerness to join the queue in the bakery and emerged clutching bags of hot, fragrant croissants and rolls.

His own stomach rumbled and he reminded himself that he hadn't eaten anything since he'd left Milan the night before. Fast food had never interested him. He preferred to wait for the real thing. And the bakery looked like the real thing.

He needed a shower and a shave but there was no chance of that until he'd picked up the key to his accommodation and he doubted his new partner was even in the surgery yet. He glanced at his watch and decided that he just about had time to eat something and still time his arrival to see her just before she started work.

He strolled into the bakery and smiled at the pretty girl behind the counter. '*Buongiorno*—good morning.'

She glanced up and caught the smile. Her blue eyes widened in feminine appreciation. 'Hello. What can I offer you?'

It was obvious from the look in those eyes that she was prepared to offer him the moon but Gio ignored the mute invitation he saw in her eyes and studied the pastries on offer, accustomed to keeping women at a polite distance. He'd always been choosy when it came to women. Too choosy, some might say. 'What's good?'

'Oh—well…' The girl lifted a hand to her face, her

cheeks suddenly pink. 'The *pain au chocolat* is my favourite but the almond croissant is our biggest seller. Take away or eat in?'

For the first time Gio noticed the small round tables covered in cheerful blue gingham, positioned by the window at the back of the shop. 'Eat in.' It was still so early he doubted that his partner had even reached the surgery yet. 'I'll take an almond croissant and a double espresso. *Grazie.*'

He selected the table with the best view over the harbour. The coffee turned out to be exceptionally good, the croissant wickedly sweet, and by the time he'd finished the last of his breakfast he'd decided that spending the summer in this quaint little village was going to be no hardship at all.

'Are you on holiday?' The girl on the till was putting croissants into bags faster than the chef could take them from the oven and still the queue didn't seem to diminish.

Gio dug his hand into his pocket and paid the bill. 'Not on holiday.' Although a holiday would have been welcome, he mused, his eyes still on the boats bobbing in the harbour. 'I'm working.'

'Working?' She handed him change. 'Where?'

'Here. I'm a doctor. A GP, to be precise.' It still felt strange to him to call himself that. For years he'd been a surgeon and he still considered himself to be a surgeon. But fate had decreed otherwise.

'You're our new doctor?'

He nodded, aware that after driving through the night he didn't exactly look the part. He could have been evasive, of course, but his new role in the community was hardly likely to remain a secret for long in a place this small. And, anyway, he didn't believe in being evasive. What was the harm in announcing himself? 'Having told you that, I might as well take advantage of your local knowledge. How does Dr Anderson take her coffee?'

All that he knew about his new partner was what David had shared in their brief phone conversation. He knew that she was married to her job, very academic and extremely serious. Already he'd formed an image of her in his mind. Tweed skirt, flat heels, horn-rimmed glasses—he knew the type. Had met plenty like her in medical school.

'Dr Anderson? That's easy.' The girl smiled, her eyes fixed on his face in a kind of trance. 'Same as you. Strong and black.'

'Ah.' His new partner was obviously a woman of taste. 'And what does she eat?'

The girl continued to gaze at him and then seemed to shake herself. 'Eat? Actually, I've never seen her eat anything.' She shrugged. 'Between the tourists and the locals, we probably keep her too busy to give her time to eat. Or maybe she isn't that interested in food.'

Gio winced and hoped it was the former. He couldn't imagine developing a good working partnership with someone who wasn't interested in food. 'In that case, I'll play it safe and take her a large Americano.' Time enough to persuade her of the benefits of eating. 'So the next thing you can do is direct me to the surgery. Or maybe Dr Anderson won't be there yet.'

It wasn't even eight o'clock.

Perhaps she slept late, or maybe—

'Follow the street right down to the harbour and it's

straight in front of you. Blue door. And she'll be there.' The girl pressed a cap onto the coffee-cup. 'She was up half the night with the Bennetts' six-year-old. Asthma attack.'

Gio lifted an eyebrow. 'You know that?'

The girl shrugged and blew a strand of hair out of her eyes. 'Around here, everyone knows everything.' She handed him the coffee and his change. 'Word gets around.'

'So maybe she's having a lie-in.'

The girl looked at the clock. 'I doubt it. Dr Anderson doesn't sleep much and, anyway, surgery starts soon.'

Gio digested that piece of information with interest. If she worked that hard, no wonder she took her coffee strong and black.

With a parting smile at the girl he left the bakery and followed her instructions, enjoying the brief walk down the steep cobbled street, glancing into shop windows as he passed.

The harbour was bigger than he'd expected, crowded with boats that bobbed and danced under the soft seduction of the sea. Tall masts clinked in the soft breeze and across the harbour he saw a row of shops and a blue door with a brass nameplate. The surgery.

A few minutes later he pushed open the surgery door and blinked in surprise. What had promised to be a small, cramped building proved to be light, airy and spacious. Somehow he'd expected something entirely different—somewhere dark and tired, like some of the surgeries he'd visited in London. What he hadn't expected was this bright, calming environment designed to soothe and relax.

Above his head glass panels threw light across a neat waiting room and on the far side of the room a children's corner overflowed with an abundance of toys in bright primary colours. A table in a glaring, cheerful red was laid with pens and sheets of paper to occupy busy hands.

On the walls posters encouraged patients to give up smoking and have their blood pressure checked and there were leaflets on first aid and adverts for various local clinics.

It seemed that nothing had been forgotten.

Gio was just studying a poster in greater depth when he noticed the receptionist.

She was bent over the curved desk, half-hidden from view as she sifted through a pile of results. Her honey blonde hair fell to her shoulders and her skin was creamy smooth and untouched by sun. She was impossibly slim, wore no make-up and the shadows under her eyes suggested that she worked harder than she should. She looked fragile, tired and very young.

Gio's eyes narrowed in an instinctively masculine assessment.

She was beautiful, he decided, and as English as scones and cream. His eyes rested on her cheekbones and then dropped to her perfectly shaped, soft mouth. He found himself thinking of summer fruit—strawberries, raspberries, redcurrants...

Something flickered to life inside him.

The girl was so absorbed in what she was reading that she hadn't even noticed him and he was just about to step forward and introduce himself when the surgery door swung open again and a group of teenage boys stumbled in, swearing and laughing.

They didn't notice him. In fact, they seemed incapable of noticing anyone, they were so drunk.

Gio stood still, sensing trouble. His dark eyes were suddenly watchful and he set the coffee down on the nearest table just in case he was going to need his hands.

One of them swore fluently as he crashed into a low table and sent magazines flying across the floor. 'Where the hell's the doctor in this place? Matt's bleeding.'

The friend in question lurched forward, blood streaming from a cut on his head. His chest was bare and he wore a pair of surf shorts, damp from the sea and bloodstained. 'Went surfing.' He gave a hiccup and tried to stand up without support but failed. Instead he slumped against his friend with a groan, his eyes closed. 'Feel sick.'

'Surfing when you're drunk is never the best idea.' The girl behind the desk straightened and looked them over with weary acceptance. Clearly it wasn't the first time she'd had drunks in the surgery. 'Sit him down over there and I'll take a look at it.'

'You?' The third teenager swaggered across the room, fingers tucked into the pockets of his jeans. He gave a suggestive wink. 'I'm Jack. How about taking a look at me while you're at it?' He leaned across the desk, leering. 'There are bits of me you might be interested in. You a nurse? You ever wear one of those blue outfits with a short skirt and stockings?'

'I'm the doctor.' The girl's eyes were cool as she pulled on a pair of disposable gloves and walked round the desk without giving Jack a second glance. 'Sit your friend down before he falls down and does himself more damage. I'll take a quick look at him before I start surgery.'

Gio didn't know who was more surprised—him or the teenagers.

She was the doctor?

She was Alice Anderson?

He ran a hand over the back of his neck and wondered why David had omitted to mention that his new partner was stunning. He tried to match up David's description of a serious, academic woman with this slender, delicate beauty standing in front of him, and failed dismally. He realised suddenly that he'd taken 'single' to mean 'mature'. And 'academic' to mean 'dowdy'.

'*You're* the doctor?' Jack lurched towards her, his gait so unsteady that he could barely stand. 'Well, that's good news. I love a woman with brains and looks. You and I could make a perfect team, babe.'

She didn't spare him a glance, refusing to respond to the banter. 'Sit your friend down.' Her tone was firm and the injured boy collapsed onto the nearest chair with a groan.

'I'll sit myself down. Oh, man, my head is killing me.'

'That's what happens when you drink all night and then bang your head.' Efficient and businesslike, she pushed up the sleeves of her plain blue top, tilted his head and took a look at the cut. She parted the boy's hair gently and probed with her fingers. Her mouth tightened. 'Well, you've done a good job of that. Were you knocked out?'

Gio cast a professional eye over the cut and saw immediately that it wasn't going to be straightforward. Surely she wasn't planning to stitch that herself? He could see ragged edges and knew it was going to be difficult to get a good cosmetic result, even for someone skilled in that area.

'I wasn't knocked out.' The teenager tried to shake

his head and instantly winced at the pain. 'I swallowed half the ocean, though. Got any aspirin?'

'In a minute. That's a nasty cut you've got there and it's near your eye and down your cheek. It's beyond my skills, I'm afraid.' She ripped off the gloves and took a few steps backwards, a slight frown on her face as she considered the options. 'You need to go to the accident and emergency department up the coast. They'll get a surgeon to stitch you up. I'll call them and let them know that you're coming.'

'No way. We haven't got time for that.' The third teenager, who hadn't spoken up until now, stepped up to her, his expression threatening. 'You're going to do it. And you're going to do it here. Right now.'

She dropped the gloves into a bin and washed her hands. 'I'll put a dressing on it for you, but you need to go to the hospital to get it stitched. They'll do a better job than I ever could. Stitching faces is an art.'

She turned to walk back across the reception area but the teenager called Jack blocked her path.

'I've got news for you, babe.' His tone was low and insulting. 'We're not going anywhere until you've fixed Matt's face. I'm not wasting a whole day of my holiday sitting in some hospital with a load of sickos. He doesn't mind a scar. Scars are sexy. Hard. You know?'

'Whoever does it, he'll be left with a scar,' she said calmly, 'but he'll get a better result at the hospital.'

'No hospital.' The boy took a step closer and stabbed a finger into her chest. 'Are you listening to me?'

'I'm listening to you but I don't think you're listening to me.' The girl didn't flinch. 'Unless he wants to have a significant scar, that cut needs to be stitched by someone with specific skills. It's for his own good.'

It happened so quickly that no one could have anticipated it. The teenager backed her against the wall and put a hand round her throat. 'I don't think you're listening to me, babe. It's your bloody job, Doc. Stitch him up! *Do it.*'

Gio crossed the room in two strides, just as the teenager uttered a howl of pain and collapsed onto the floor in a foetal position, clutching his groin.

She'd kneed him.

'Don't try and tell me my job.' She lifted her hand to her reddened throat. Her tone was chilly and composed and then she glanced up, noticed Gio for the first time and her face visibly paled. For a moment she just stared at him and then her gaze flickered towards the door, measuring the distance. Gio winced inwardly. It was obvious that she thought he was trouble and he felt slightly miffed by her reaction.

He liked women. Women liked him. And they usually responded to him. They chatted, they flirted, they sent him long looks. The look in Dr Anderson's eyes suggested that she was calculating ways to injure him. All right, so he hadn't had time to shave and change, but did he really look that scary?

He was about to introduce himself, about to try and redeem himself in her eyes, when the third teenager stepped towards the girl, his expression threatening. Gio closed a hand over his arm and yanked him backwards.

'I think it's time you left. Both of you.' His tone was icy cool and he held the boy in an iron grip. 'You can pick up your friend in an hour.'

The teenager balled his fists, prepared to fight, but then eyed the width of Gio's shoulders. His hands relaxed and he gave a slight frown. 'Whazzit to do with you?'

'Everything.' Gio stepped forward so that his body was between them and Dr Anderson. 'I work here.'

'What as?' The boy twisted in his grip and his eyes slid from Gio's shoulders to the hard line of his jaw. 'A bouncer?'

'A doctor. One hour. That's how long I estimate it's going to take to make a decent job of his face. Or you can drive to the hospital.' Gio released him, aware that Alice was staring at him in disbelief. 'Your choice.'

The teenager winced and rubbed his arm. 'She…' he jerked his head towards the doctor '…said he needed a specialist doctor.'

'Well, this is your lucky day, because I am a specialist doctor.'

There was a long pause while the teenager tried to focus. 'You don't look anything like a doctor. Doctors shave and dress smart. You look more like one of those—those…' His words slurred and he swayed and waved a hand vaguely. 'Those Mafia thugs that you see in films.'

'Then you'd better behave yourself,' Gio suggested silkily, casting a glance towards his new partner to check she was all right. Her pallor was worrying him. He hoped she wasn't about to pass out. 'Leave now and come back in an hour for your friend.'

'You're not English.' The boy hiccoughed. 'What are you, then? Italian?'

'I'm Sicilian.' Gio's eyes were cold. '*Never* call me Italian.'

'Sicilian?' A nervous respect entered the teenager's eyes and he licked his lips and eyed the door. 'OK.' He gave a casual shrug. 'So maybe we'll come back later, like you suggested.'

Gio nodded. 'Good decision.'

The boy backed away, still rubbing his arm. 'We're going. C'mon, Rick.' He loped over to the door and left without a backward glance.

'*Dios,* did he hurt you?' Gio walked over to the girl and lifted a hand to her neck. The skin was slightly reddened and he stroked a finger carefully over the bruising with a frown. 'We should call the police now.'

She shook her head and backed away. 'No need. He didn't hurt me.' She glanced towards the teenager who was still sprawled over the seats of her waiting room and gave a wry shake of her head. 'If you're Dr Moretti, we'd better see to him before he's sick on the floor or bleeds to death over my chairs.'

'It won't hurt him to wait for two minutes. You should call the police.' Gio's tone was firm. He didn't want to be too graphic about what might have happened, but it was important that she acknowledge the danger. It hadn't escaped him that if he hadn't decided to arrive at the surgery early, she would have been on her own with them. 'You should call them.'

She rubbed her neck. 'I suppose you're right. All right, I'll do it when I get a minute.'

'Does this happen often? I imagined I was coming to a quiet seaside village. Not some hotbed of violence.'

'There's nothing quiet about this place, at least not in the middle of summer,' she said wearily. 'We're the only doctors' surgery in this part of the town and the nearest A and E is twenty miles down the coast so, yes, we get our fair share of drama. David probably didn't tell you that when he was persuading you to take the job. You can leave now, if you like.'

His eyes rested on her soft mouth. 'I'm not leaving.'

There was a brief silence. A silence during which she stared back at him. Then she licked her lips. 'Well, that's good news for my patients. And good news for me. I'm glad you arrived when you did.'

'You didn't look glad.'

'Well, a girl can't be too careful and you don't exactly look like a doctor.' A hint of a smile touched that perfect mouth. 'Did you see his face when you said you were Sicilian? I think they were expecting you to put a hand in your jacket and shoot them dead any moment.'

'I considered it.' Gio's eyes gleamed with humour. 'But I've only had one cup of coffee so far today. Generally I need at least two before I shoot people dead. And you don't need to apologise for the mistake. I confess that I thought you were the receptionist. If you're Alice Anderson, you're nothing like David's description.'

'I can imagine.' She spoke in a tone of weary acceptance. 'David is seeing the world through a romantic haze at the moment. Be patient with him. It will pass, given time.'

He laughed. 'You think so?'

'Love always does, Dr Moretti. Like many viruses, it's a self-limiting condition. Left alone, the body can cure itself.'

Gio searched her face to see if she was joking and decided that she wasn't. Filing the information away in his brain for later use, he walked over to retrieve the coffee from the window-sill. 'If you're truly Dr Anderson, this is for you. An ice breaker, from me.'

She stared at the coffee with sudden hunger in her eyes and then at him. 'You brought coffee?' Judging from the expression on her face, he might have offered her an expensive bauble from Tiffany's. She lifted a hand and brushed a strand of hair out of her eyes. Tired eyes. 'For me? Is it black?'

'*Si.*' He smiled easily and handed her the coffee, amused by her response. 'You have fans in the bakery who know every detail of your dietary preferences. I was told "just coffee" so I passed on the croissant.'

'There's no such thing as "just coffee". Coffee is wonderful. It's my only vice and currently I'm in desperate need of a caffeine hit.' She prised the lid off the coffee, sniffed and gave a whimper of pleasure. 'Large Americano. Oh, that's just the best smell…'

He watched as she sipped, closed her eyes and savoured the taste. She gave a tiny moan of appreciation that sent a flicker of awareness through his body. He gave a slight frown at the strength of his reaction.

'So…' She studied him for a moment and then took another sip of coffee. Some of the colour returned to her cheeks. 'I wasn't expecting you until tomorrow. Not that I'm complaining, you understand. I'm glad you're early. You were just in time to save me from a nasty situation.'

'I prefer to drive when the roads are clear. I thought you might appreciate the help, given that David has already been gone two days. We haven't been formally introduced. I'm Gio Moretti.' He wanted to hold her until she stopped shaking but he sensed that she wouldn't appreciate the gesture so he kept his distance. 'I'm your new partner.'

She hesitated and then put her free hand in his. 'Alice Anderson.'

'I gathered that. You're really *not* what I expected.'

She tilted her head to one side. 'You're standing in my surgery having frightened off two teenage thugs by your appearance and you're telling me *I'm* not what *you* expected?' There was a hint of humour in her blue eyes and his attention was caught by the length of her lashes.

'So maybe I don't fit anyone's image of a conventional doctor right at this moment...' he dragged his gaze away from her face and glanced down at himself with a rueful smile '...but I've been travelling all night and I'm dressed for comfort. After a shave and a quick change of clothes, I will be ready to impress your patients. But first show me to a room and I'll stitch that boy before his friends return.'

'Are you sure?' She frowned slightly. 'I mean, David told me you didn't operate any more and—'

'I don't operate.' He waited for the usual feelings to rise up inside him. Waited for the frustration and the sick disappointment. Nothing happened. Maybe he was just tired. Or maybe he'd made progress. 'I don't operate, but I can certainly stitch up a face.'

'Then I'm very grateful and I'm certainly not going to argue with you. That wound is beyond my skills and I've got a full surgery starting in ten minutes.' She looked at the teenager who was sprawled across the chairs, eyes closed, and sighed. 'Oh, joy. Is it alcohol or a bang on the head, do you think?'

'Hard to tell.' Gio followed her gaze and shook his head slowly. 'I'll stitch him up, do a neurological assessment and then we'll see. Is there anyone who can help me? Show me around? I can give you a list of what I'll need.'

'Rita, our practice nurse, will be here in a minute. She's very experienced. Her asthma clinic doesn't start until ten so I'll send her in.' Her eyes slid over him. 'Are you sure you're all right with this? We weren't expecting you until tomorrow and if you've been travelling all night you must be tired.'

'I'm fine.' He studied her carefully, noting the dark shadows under her eyes. 'In fact, I'd say that you're the one who's tired, Dr Anderson.'

She gave a dismissive shrug. 'Goes with the job. I'll show you where you can work. We have a separate room for minor surgery. I think you'll find everything you need but I can't be sure. We don't usually stitch faces.'

He followed her down the corridor, his eyes drawn to the gentle swing of her hips. 'Do you have 5/0 Ethilon?'

'Yes.' She pushed open a door and held it open while he walked inside. 'Is that all you need?'

'The really important thing is to debride the wound and align the tissues exactly. And not leave the stitches in for too long.'

Her glance was interested. Intelligent. 'I wish I had time to watch you. Not that I'm about to start suturing faces,' she assured him hastily, and he smiled.

'Like most things, it's just a question of practice.'

She opened a cupboard. 'Stitches are in here. Gloves on the shelf. You're probably about the same size as David. Tetanus et cetera in the fridge.' She waved a hand. 'I'll send Rita in with the patient. I'll get on with surgery. Come and find me when you've finished.'

'Alice.' He stopped her before she walked out of the door. 'Don't forget to call the police.'

She tilted her head back and he sensed that she was wrestling with what seemed like a major inconvenience then she gave a resigned sigh.

'I'll do that.'

CHAPTER TWO

ALICE spoke to Rita, called the police and then worked flat out, seeing patients, with no time to even think about checking on her new partner.

'How long have you had this rash on your eye, Mr Denny?' As she saw her tenth patient of the morning, she thought gratefully of the cup of coffee that Gio Moretti had thought to bring her. It was the only sustenance she'd had all day.

'It started with a bit of pain and tingling. Then it all went numb.' The man sat still as she examined him. 'I suppose all that began on Saturday. My wife noticed the rash yesterday. She was worried because it looks blistered. We wondered if I'd brushed up against something in the garden. You know how it is with some of those plants.'

Alice picked up her ophthalmoscope and examined his eye thoroughly. 'I don't think it's anything to do with the garden, Mr Denny. You've got quite a discharge from your eye.'

'It's very sore.'

'I'm sure it is.' Alice put the ophthalmoscope down on her desk and washed her hands. 'I want to test your vision. Can you read the letters for me?'

The man squinted at the chart on her wall and struggled to recite the letters. 'Not very clear, I'm afraid.' He looked worried. 'My eyes have always been good. Am I losing my sight?'

'You have a virus.' Alice sat down and tapped something into her computer. Then she turned back to the patient. 'I think you have shingles, Mr Denny.'

'Shingles?' He frowned. 'In my eye?'

'Shingles is a virus that affects the nerves,' she explained, 'and one in five cases occur in the eye—to be technical, it's the ophthalmic branch of the trigeminal nerve.'

He pulled a face. 'Never was much good at biology.'

Alice smiled. 'You don't need biology, Mr Denny. But I just wanted you to know it isn't uncommon, unfortunately. I'm going to need to refer you to an ophthalmologist—an eye doctor at the hospital. Is there someone who can take you up there?'

He nodded. 'My daughter's waiting in the car park. She brought me here.'

'Good.' Alice reached for the phone and dialled the clinic number. 'They'll see you within the next couple of days.'

'Do I really need to go there?'

Alice nodded. 'They need to examine your eye with a slit lamp—a special piece of equipment that allows them to look at your eye properly. They need to exclude iritis. In the meantime, I'll give you aciclovir to take five times a day for a week. It should speed up healing time and reduce the incidence of new lesions.' She printed out the prescription on the computer as she waited for the hospital to answer the phone.

Once she'd spoken to the consultant, she quickly

wrote a letter and gave it to the patient. 'They're really nice up there,' she assured him, 'but if you have any worries you're welcome to come back to me.'

He left the room and Alice picked up a set of results. She was studying the numbers with a puzzled frown when Rita walked in. A motherly woman in her early fifties, her navy blue uniform was stretched over her large bosom and there was a far-away expression on her face. 'Pinch me. Go on, pinch me hard. I've died and gone to heaven.'

Alice looked up. 'Rita, have you seen Mrs Frank lately? I ran some tests but the results just don't make sense.' She'd examined the patient carefully and had been expecting something entirely different. She studied the results again. Perhaps she'd missed something.

'Forget Mrs Frank's results for a moment.' Rita closed the door behind her. 'I've got something far more important for you to think about.'

Alice didn't look up. 'I thought she had hypothyroidism. She had all the symptoms.'

'Alice…'

Still absorbed in the problem, Alice shook her head. 'The results are normal.' She checked the results one more time and checked the normal values, just in case she'd missed something. She'd been so *sure*.

'*Alice!*' Rita sounded exasperated. 'Are you even listening to me?'

Alice dragged her eyes away from the piece of paper in her hand, still pondering. Aware that Rita was glaring at her, she gave a faint smile. 'Sorry, I'm still thinking about Mrs Frank,' she admitted apologetically. 'What's the matter?'

'Dr Giovanni Moretti is the matter.'

'Oh, my goodness!' Alice slapped her hand over her mouth and rose to her feet quickly, ridden with guilt. 'I'd *totally* forgotten about him. How could I?'

Rita stared at her. 'How could you, indeed?'

'Don't! I feel terrible about it.' Guilt consumed her. And after he'd been so helpful. 'How could I have done that? I showed him into the room, made sure he had what he needed and I *promised* to look in on him, but I've had streams of patients this morning and I completely forgot his existence.'

'You forgot his existence?' Rita shook her head. 'Alice, how could you *possibly* have forgotten his existence?'

'I know, it's dreadful! I feel terribly rude.' She walked briskly round her desk, determined to make amends. 'I'll go and check on him immediately. Hopefully, if he'd needed any help he would have come and found me.'

'Help?' Rita's tone was dry. 'Trust me, Alice, the guy doesn't need any help from you or anyone else. He's slick. Mr Hotshot. Or I suppose I should call him Dr Hotshot.'

'He's finished stitching the boy?' She glanced at her watch for the first time since she'd started surgery and realised with a shock that almost an hour and a half had passed.

'Just the head, although personally I would have been happy to see him do the mouth as well.' Rita gave a snort of disapproval. 'Never heard such obscenities.'

'Yes, they were pretty drunk, the three of them. How does the head look?'

'Better than that boy deserves. Never seen a job as neat in my life and I've been nursing for thirty years,'

Rita admitted, a dreamy expression on her face. 'Dr Moretti has *amazing* hands.'

'He used to be a surgeon. If he's done a good job and he's finished, why did you come rushing in here telling me he was having problems?'

'I never said he was having problems.'

'You said something was the matter.'

'No.' Rita closed her eyes and sighed. 'At least, not with him. Only with me. I think he's fantastic.'

'Oh.' Alice paused by the door. 'Well, he arrived a day early, brought me coffee first thing, sorted out a bunch of rowdy teenagers and stitched a nasty cut so, yes, I think he's fantastic, too. He's obviously a good doctor.'

'I'm not talking about his medical skills, Alice.'

'What are you talking about, then?'

'Alice, he's *gorgeous*. Don't tell me you haven't noticed!'

'Actually, I thought he looked a mess.' Her hand dropped from the doorhandle and she frowned at the recollection. 'But he'd been travelling all night.'

'A mess?' Rita sounded faint. 'You think he looks a *mess?*'

Alice wondered whether to confess that she'd thought he looked dangerous. Strangely enough, the teenagers hadn't bothered her. They were nothing more than gawky children and she'd had no doubts about her ability to handle them. But when she'd looked up and seen Gio standing there…

'I'm sure he'll look more respectable when he's had a shower and a shave.' Alice frowned. 'And possibly a haircut. The boy was in such a state, I didn't think it mattered.'

'You didn't even notice, did you?' Rita shook her head in disbelief. 'Alice, you need to do something about your life. The man is sex on a stick. He's a walking female fantasy.'

Alice stared at her blankly, struggling to understand. 'Rita, you've been married for twenty years and, anyway, he's far too young for you.'

Rita gave her a suggestive wink. 'Don't you believe it. I like them young and vigorous.'

Alice sighed and wished she didn't feel so completely out of step with the rest of her sex. Was she the only woman in the world who didn't spend her whole life thinking about men? Even Rita was susceptible, even though she'd reached an age where she should have grown out of such stupidity.

'He doesn't look much like a doctor,' she said frankly, 'but I'm sure he'll look better once he's shaved and changed his clothes.'

'He looks every inch a man. And he'd be perfect for you.'

Alice froze. 'I refuse to have this conversation with you again, Rita. And while we're at it, you can tell that receptionist of ours that I'm not having it with her either.'

Rita sniffed. 'Mary worries about you, as I do, and—'

'I'm not interested in men and both of you know that.'

'Well, you should be.' Rita folded her arms and her mouth clamped into a thin line. 'You're thirty years of age and—'

'Rita!' Alice interrupted her sharply. 'This is not a good time.'

'It's never a good time with you. You never talk about it.'

'Because there's nothing to talk about!' Alice took a deep breath. 'I appreciate your concern, really, but—'

'But you're married to your work and that's the way you're staying.' The older woman rose to her feet and Alice sighed.

'I'm happy, Rita.' Her voice softened slightly as she saw the worry in the older woman's face. 'Really I am. I like my life the way it is.'

'Empty, you mean.'

'Empty?' Alice laughed and stroked blonde hair away from her face. 'Rita, I'm so busy I don't have time to turn round. My life certainly isn't empty.'

Rita pursed her lips. 'You're talking about work and work isn't enough for anybody. A woman needs a social life. A man. Sex.'

Alice glanced pointedly at her watch. 'Was there anything else you wanted to talk about? I've got a surgery full of patients, Rita.'

And she was exhausted, hungry and thirsty and fed up with talking about subjects that didn't interest her.

'All right. I can take a hint. But the subject isn't closed.' Rita walked to the door. 'Actually, I did come to ask you something. Although he doesn't need your help, Gio wants two minutes to discuss the boy with you before he sends him out. Oh, and the police are here.'

Alice stood up and removed a bottle of water from the fridge in her consulting room. She couldn't do anything about the hunger, but at least she could drink. 'I don't have time for them right now.'

'If what Gio told me is correct, you're going to make time.' Suddenly Rita was all business. 'They can't go round behaving like that. And you need to lock the door behind you if you come in early in the morning. You might have been the only person in the building. You were careless. Up half the night with the little Bennett girl and not getting enough sleep as usual, no doubt.'

'Rita—'

'You'll tell me I'm nagging but I worry about you, that's all. I care about you.'

'I know you do.' Alice curled her hands into fists, uncomfortable with the conversation. Another person—*a different person to her*—would have swept across to Rita and given her a big hug, but Alice could no more do that than fly. Touching wasn't part of her nature. 'I know you care.'

'Good.' Rita gave a sniff. 'Now, drink your water before you die of dehydration and then go and see Gio. And this time take a closer look. You might like what you see.'

Alice walked back to her desk and poured water into a glass. 'All right, I'll speak to Gio then I'll see the police. Ask Mary to give them a coffee and put them in one of the empty rooms. Then see if she can placate the remaining patients. Tell them I'll be with them as soon as possible.' She paused to drink the water she'd poured and then set the glass on her desk. 'Goodness knows if I'll get through them all in time to do any house calls.'

'Gio is going to help you see the patients once he's discharged the boy. For goodness' sake, don't say no. It's like the first day of the summer sales in the waiting room. If he helps then we might all stand a chance of getting some lunch.'

'The letting agent is dropping the keys to his flat round here. He needs to get settled in. He needs to rest after the journey and shave the designer stubble—'

'Any fool can see he's a man with stamina and I don't see his appearance hampering his ability to see patients,' Rita observed, with impeccable logic. 'We're just ensuring that the surgery is going to be crammed for weeks to come.'

'Why's that?'

'Because he's too gorgeous for his own good and all the women in the practice are going to want to come and stare.'

Alice opened the door. 'What exactly is it about men that turns normally sane women into idiots?' she wondered out loud, and Rita grinned.

'Whoever said I was sane?'

With an exasperated shake of her head, Alice walked along the corridor and pushed open the door of the room they used for minor surgery. 'Dr Moretti, I'm so sorry, I've had a steady stream of patients and I lost track of the time.'

He turned to look at her and for a brief, unsettling moment Alice remembered Rita's comment about him being a walking fantasy. He was handsome, she conceded, in an intelligent, devilish and slightly dangerous way. She could see that some women would find him attractive. Fortunately she wasn't one of them.

'No problem.' His smile came easily. 'I've just finished here. I don't need anyone to hold my hand.'

'Shame,' Rita breathed, and Alice shot her a look designed to silence.

Gio ripped off his gloves and pushed the trolley away from him. 'I think he's safe to discharge. He wasn't knocked out and his consciousness isn't impaired. Fortunately he obviously drank less than his friends. I see no indication for an X-ray or a CT scan at the moment.

He can be discharged with a head injury form.' He turned to the boy, his expression serious. 'I advise you to stay off the alcohol for a few days. If you start vomiting, feel drowsy, confused, have any visual disturbances or experience persistent headache within the next forty-eight hours, you should go to the A and E department at the hospital. Either way, you need those stitches out in four days. Don't forget and don't think it's cool to leave them in.'

The boy gave a nod and slid off the couch, his face ashen. 'Yeah. I hear you. Thanks, Doc. Are the guys outside?'

'They're having a cosy chat with the police,' Rita told him sweetly, and the boy flushed and rubbed a hand over his face.

'Man, I'm sorry about that.' He shook his head and breathed out heavily. 'They were a bit the worse for wear. We were at an all-night beach party.' He glanced sideways at Alice, his expression sheepish. 'You OK?'

She nodded. 'I'm fine.' She was busy looking at the wound. She couldn't believe how neat the sutures were.

The boy left the room, escorted by Rita.

'You did an amazing job, thank you so much.' Alice closed the door behind them and turned to Gio. 'I never would have thought that was possible. That cut looked such a mess. So many ragged edges. I wouldn't have known where to start.'

But obviously he'd known exactly where to start. Despite appearances. If she hadn't seen the results of his handiwork with her own eyes, she would still have struggled to believe that he was a doctor.

When David had described his friend, she'd imagined

a smooth, slick Italian in a designer suit. Someone safe, conservative and conventional in appearance and attitude.

There was nothing safe or conservative about Gio.

He hovered on the wrong side of respectable. His faded T-shirt was stretched over shoulders that were both broad and muscular and a pair of equally faded jeans hugged his legs. His face was deeply tanned, his jaw dark with stubble and his eyes held a hard watchfulness that suggested no small degree of life experience.

She tried to imagine him dressed in a more conventional manner, and failed.

'He'll have a scar.' Gio tipped the remains of his equipment into the nearest sharps bin. 'But some of it will be hidden by his hair. I gather from Rita that you have a very long queue out there.'

Remembering the patients, exhaustion suddenly washed over her and she sucked in a breath, wondering for a moment how she was going to get through the rest of the day. 'I need to talk to the police and then get back to work. I'm sorry I don't have time to give you a proper tour. Hopefully I can do that tomorrow, before you officially start.'

'Forget the tour.' His eyes scanned her face. 'You look done in. The girl who made your coffee told me that you were up in the night, dealing with an asthma attack. You must be ready for a rest yourself. Let's split the rest of the patients.'

She gave a wan smile. 'I can't ask you to do that. You've been travelling all night.' It occurred to her that he was the one who ought to look tired. Instead, his gaze was sharp, assessing.

'You're not asking, I'm offering. In fact, I'm insisting. If you drop dead from overwork before this afternoon, who will show me round?'

His smile had a relaxed, easy charm and she found herself responding. 'Well, if you're sure. I'll ask Mary to send David's patients through to you. If you need any help just buzz me. Lift the receiver and press 3.'

CHAPTER THREE

'WHAT a day!' Seven hours later, Gio rubbed a hand over his aching shoulder and eyed the waiting room warily. Morning surgery had extended into the afternoon well-woman clinic, which had extended into evening surgery. Even now the telephone rang incessantly, two little boys were playing noisily in the play corner and a harassed-looking woman was standing at the reception desk, wiggling a pram in an attempt to soothe a screaming baby. 'I feel as though I have seen the entire population of Cornwall in one surgery. Is it always like this?'

'No, sometimes it's busy.' Mary, the receptionist, replaced the phone once again and gave him a cheerful smile as she flicked through the box of repeat prescriptions for the waiting mother. 'Don't worry, you get used to it after a while. I could try locking the door but it would only postpone the inevitable. They'd all be back tomorrow. There we are, Mrs York.' She handed over a prescription with a flourish and adjusted her glasses more comfortably on her nose. 'How are those twins of yours doing, Harriet? Behaving themselves?'

The young woman glanced towards the boys, her

face pale. 'They're fine.' Her tone had an edge to it as she pushed the prescription into her handbag. 'Thanks.'

The baby's howls intensified and Mary stood up, clucking. She was a plump, motherly woman with curling hair a soft shade of blonde and a smiling face. Gio could see that she was dying to get her hands on the baby. 'There, now. What a fuss. Libby York, what do you think you're doing to our eardrums and your poor mother's sanity?' She walked round the reception desk, glanced at the baby's mother for permission and then scooped the baby out of the pram and rested it on her shoulder, cooing and soothing. 'Is she sleeping for you, dear?' Despite the attention, the baby continued to bawl and howl and Harriet gritted her teeth.

'Not much. She—' The young woman broke off as the boys started to scrap over a toy. 'Stop it, you two!' Her tone was sharp. 'Dan! Robert! Come here, now! Oh, for heaven's sake…' She closed her eyes and swallowed hard.

The baby continued to scream and Gio caught Mary's eye and exchanged a look of mutual understanding. 'Let me have a try.' He took the baby from her, his touch firm and confident, his voice deep and soothing as he switched to Italian. The baby stopped yelling, hiccoughed a few times and then calmed and stared up at his face in fascination.

At least one woman still found him interesting in a dishevelled state, he thought with a flash of amusement as he recalled Alice's reaction to his appearance.

Mary gave a sigh of relief and turned to Harriet. 'There. That's better. She wanted a man's strength.' She put a hand on the young mother's arm. It was a comforting touch. 'It's hard when they're this age. I remember when mine were small, there were days when I thought I'd strangle them all. It gets easier. Before you know it they're grown.'

Harriet looked at her and blinked back tears. Then she covered her mouth with her hand and shook her head. 'Sorry—oh, I'm being so stupid!' Her hand dropped and she sniffed. 'It's just that I don't know what to do with them half the time. Or what to do with me. I'm so tired I can't think straight,' she muttered, glancing towards the baby who was now calm in Gio's arms. 'This one's keeping the whole family awake. It makes us all cranky and those two are so naughty I could—' She broke off and caught her lip between her teeth. 'Anyway, as you say, it's all part of them being small. There's going to come a time when I'll wish they were little again.'

With a forced smile and a nod of thanks, she leaned across and took the baby from Gio.

'How old is the baby?' There was something about the woman that was worrying him. He didn't know her, of course, which didn't help, but still…

'She'll be seven weeks tomorrow.' Harriet jiggled the baby in her arms in an attempt to keep her calm.

'It can be very hard. My sister had her third child two months ago,' Gio said, keeping his tone casual, 'and she's certainly struggling. If the baby keeps crying, bring her to see me. Maybe there's something we can do to help.'

'Dr Moretti has taken over from Dr Watts,' Mary explained, and Harriet nodded.

'OK. Thanks. I'd better be getting back home. She needs feeding.'

'I can make you comfortable in a room here,' Mary

offered, but the woman shook her head and walked towards the door, juggling pram and baby.

'I'd better get home. I've got beds to change and washing to put out.' She called to the boys, who ignored her. 'Come on!' They still ignored her and she gave a growl of exasperation and strapped the baby back in the pram. Libby immediately started crying again. 'Yes, I know, I know! I'm getting you home right now!' She glared at the twins. 'If you don't come now I'm leaving you both here.' Her voice rose slightly and she reached out and grabbed the nearest boy by the arm. 'Do as you're told.'

They left the surgery, boys arguing, baby crying. Mary stared after them, her fingers drumming a steady rhythm on the desk. 'I don't like the look of that.'

'No.' Gio was in full agreement. There had been something about the young mother that had tugged at him. 'She looked stretched out. At her limit.'

Mary looked at him. 'You think there's something wrong with the baby?'

'No. I think there's something wrong with the mother, but I didn't want to get into a conversation that personal with a woman I don't know in the reception area. A conversation like that requires sensitivity. One wrong word and she would have run.'

'Finally. A man who thinks before he speaks…' Mary gave a sigh of approval and glanced up as Alice walked out of her consulting room, juggling two empty coffee-cups and an armful of notes.

She looked even paler than she had that morning, Gio noted, but perhaps that was hardly surprising. She'd been working flat out all day with no break.

'Did I hear a baby screaming?' She deposited the notes on the desk.

'Libby York.' Mary turned her head and stared through the glass door into the street where Harriet was still struggling with the boys. As they disappeared round the corner, she turned back with a sigh. 'You were great, Dr Moretti. Any time you want to soothe my nerves with a short spurt of Italian, don't let me stop you.'

Gio gave an apologetic shrug. 'My English doesn't run to baby talk.'

Alice frowned, her mind focused on the job. 'Why was Harriet in here?'

'Picking up a repeat prescription for her husband.' Mary's mouth tightened and her eyes suddenly clouded with worry. 'I knew that girl when she was in primary school. The smile never left her face. Look at her now and her face is grim. As if she's holding it together by a thread. As if every moment is an effort. If you ask me, she's close to the edge.'

'She has three children under the age of six. Twin boys of five. It's the summer holidays so she has them at home all day.' Alice frowned slightly. Considered. 'That's hard work by anyone's standards. Her husband is a fisherman so he works pretty long hours. Her mother died a month before the baby was born and there's no other family on the scene that I'm aware of. On top of that her delivery was difficult and she had a significant post-partum haemorrhage. She had her postnatal check at the hospital with the consultant.'

She knew her patients well, Gio thought as he watched her sifting through the facts. She was making mental lists. Looking at the evidence in front of her.

'Yes.' Mary glanced at her. 'It might be that.'

'But you don't think so?'

'You want my opinion?' Mary pressed her lips together as the telephone rang yet again. 'I think she's depressed. And Dr Moretti agrees with me.'

'A new baby is hard work.'

'That's right. It is.' Mary reached out and picked up the receiver. 'Appointments line, good afternoon.' She listened and consulted the computer for an appointment slot while Alice ran a hand through her hair and turned to Gio.

'Did she seem depressed to you?'

'Hard to be sure. She seemed stressed and tired,' he conceded, wondering whether she gave all her patients this much thought and attention when they hadn't even asked for help. If so, it was no wonder she was tired and overworked.

'I'll talk to the Gina, the health visitor, and maybe I'll call round and see her at home.'

'You haven't got time to call and see everyone at home.' Mary replaced the receiver and rejoined the conversation. 'She was David's patient, which means she's now Dr Moretti's responsibility. Let him deal with it. Chances are she'll make an appointment with him in the next couple of days. If she doesn't, well, I'll just have to nudge her along.'

To Gio's surprise, Alice nodded. 'All right. But keep an eye on her, Mary.'

'Of course.'

Alice put the cups down and lifted a journal that was lying on the desk.

She had slim hands, he noticed. Delicate. Like the rest of her. It seemed unbelievable that someone so fragile-looking could handle such a punishing workload. She glanced up and caught him looking at her. 'If you want to know anything about this town or the people in it, ask Mary or Rita. They went to school together and they've lived here all their lives. They actually qualify as locals.' She dropped the journal back on the desk and looked at Mary. 'Did the letting agent drop off Dr Moretti's keys?'

'Ah—I was building up to that piece of news.' Mary pulled a face and adjusted her glasses. 'There's a slight problem with the let that David arranged.'

'What problem?'

Mary looked vague. 'They've had a misunderstanding in the office. Some junior girl didn't realise it was being reserved for Dr Moretti and gave it away to a bunch of holidaymakers.' She frowned and waved a hand. 'French, I think.'

Alice tapped her foot on the floor and her mouth tightened. 'Then they'll just have to find him something else. Fast.' She cast an apologetic glance at Gio. 'Sorry about this. You must be exhausted.'

Not as exhausted as she was, Gio mused, wondering whether she'd eaten at all during the day. Whether she ever stopped thinking about work. At some point, Rita had produced a sandwich and an excellent cup of coffee for him but that had been hours earlier and he was ready for something more substantial to eat. And a hot bath. His shoulder was aching again.

'Not that easy.' Mary checked the notes she'd made. 'Nothing is free until September. Schools are back by then. Demand falls a bit.'

'September?' Alice stared. 'But it's still only July.'

Gio studied Mary carefully. Something didn't feel quite right. She was clearly a caring, hospitable woman. Efficient, too. And yet she seemed totally unconcerned about his apparent lack of accommodation. 'You have an alternative plan?'

'Hotels,' Alice said firmly. 'We just need to ring round and see if—'

'No hotels,' Mary said immediately, sitting back in her chair and giving a helpless shrug. 'Full to the brim. We're having a good season, tourist-wise. Betty in the newsagent reckons it's been the best July since she took over from her mother in 1970.'

'Mary.' Alice's voice was exasperated. 'I don't care about the tourists and at the moment I don't care about Betty's sales figures, but I do care about Dr Moretti having somewhere to live while he's working here! You have to do something. And you have to do it right now.'

'I'm trying a few letting agents up the coast,' Mary murmured, peering over the top of her glasses, 'but I'm getting nowhere at the moment. Might need an interim plan. I know.' Her face brightened with inspiration. 'He can stay with you. Just until I find somewhere.'

There was a long silence and something flashed in Alice's eyes. Something dangerous. 'Mary.' There was an unspoken threat in her voice but Mary waved a hand airily.

'You're rattling around in that huge house in the middle of nowhere and it isn't safe at this time of year with all those weirdos on the beach and—'

'Mary!' This time her tone was sharp and she stepped closer to the desk and lowered her voice. 'Mary, don't you dare do this. Don't you *dare*.'

'Do what?'

'Interfere.' Alice gritted her teeth. 'He can't stay with me. That isn't a solution.'

'It's a perfect solution.' Mary smiled up at her innocently and Gio saw the frustration in Alice's face and wondered.

'You've gone too far this time,' she muttered. 'You're embarrassing me and you're embarrassing Dr Moretti.'

Not in the least embarrassed, Gio watched, intrigued. He wouldn't have been at all surprised if she was going to throw a punch. It was clear that she believed that Mary had in some way orchestrated the current problem.

Adding weight to his theory, the older woman looked over the top of her glasses, her gaze innocent. *Far too innocent.* 'It's the perfect solution while I look for somewhere else. Why not?'

'Well, because I…' Alice sucked in a breath and ran a hand over the back of her neck. 'You know I don't—'

'Well, now you do.' Mary beamed, refusing to back down. 'It's temporary, Alice. As a favour to the community. Can't have our new doctor sleeping rough in the gutter, can we? Are you ready to go, Rita?' She stood up as the practice nurse walked into reception. 'What a day. I'm going to pour myself a large glass of wine and put my feet up. Can we call in at Betty's on the way? I need to pick up a local paper. See you in the morning. Oh, and by the way…' She turned to Gio with a wink. 'I suggest you order a take-away for dinner. Our Dr Anderson is a whiz with patients but the kitchen isn't her forte.'

They left with a wave and Gio watched as Alice's hands clenched and unclenched by her sides.

He broke the tense silence. 'You look as though you're looking for someone to thump.'

She turned and blinked, almost as if she'd forgotten his existence. As if he wasn't part of her problem. 'Tell me something.' Her voice was tight. 'Is it really possible to admire and respect someone and yet want to strangle them at the same time?'

He thought of his sisters and nodded. 'Definitely.'

He noticed that she didn't use the word 'love' although it had taken him less than five minutes to detect the warmth and affection running between the three women.

'I want to be so *angry* with the pair of them.' Her hand sliced through the air and the movement encouraged wisps of her hair to drift over her eyes. 'But how can I when I know—' she broke off and let out a long breath, struggling for control. 'This isn't anything to do with you. What I mean is…' Her tone was suddenly tight and formal, her smile forced, 'you must think I'm incredibly rude, but that wasn't my intention. It's just that you've stepped into the middle of something that's been going on for a long time and—'

'And you don't like being set up with the first available guy who happens to walk through the door?'

Her blue eyes flew to his, startled. 'It's that obvious? Oh, this is so embarrassing.'

'Not embarrassing.' He watched as the colour flooded into her cheeks. 'But interesting. Why do your colleagues feel the need to interfere with your love life?'

She was a beautiful woman. He knew enough about men to know that a woman like her could have the male sex swarming around her without any assistance whatsoever.

She paced the length of the waiting room and back again, working off tension. 'Because people have a stereotypical view of life,' she said, her tone ringing with exasperation. 'If you're not with a man, you must want to be. Secretly you must long to be married and have eight children and a dog. And if you're not, you're viewed as some sort of freak.'

Gio winced. 'Eight is definitely too many.' He was pleased to see a glimmer of humour in her eyes.

'You think so?'

'Trust me.' He tried to coax the smile still wider. Suddenly he wanted to see her smile. Really smile. 'I am one of six and the queue for the bathroom was unbelievable. And the battle at the meal table was nothing short of ugly.'

The smile was worth waiting for. Dimples winked at the side of her soft mouth and her eyes danced. Captivated by the dimples, Gio felt something clench inside him.

She was beautiful.

And very guarded. He saw something in the depths of her blue eyes that made him wonder about her past.

Still smiling, she gave a shake of her head. 'I know they mean well but they've gone too far this time. It's even worse than that time on the lifeboat.'

'The lifeboat?'

'Believe me, you don't want to know.' She sucked in a breath and raked slim fingers through her silky blonde hair. 'Let's look at this logically. I'm assuming Mary was telling the truth about your flat having fallen through—'

'You think she might have been lying?'

'Not lying, no. But she's manoeuvred it in some way. I don't know how yet, but when I find out she's going to be in trouble. Either way, at the moment, it looks as though you're going to have to stay with me. Aggh!' She tilted her head backwards and made a frustrated sound. 'And I'll never hear the last of it! Every morning they're going to be looking at me, working out whether I've fallen in love with you yet. Nudging. Making comments. I'll kill them.'

He couldn't keep the laughter out of his voice. 'Is that what you're afraid of? Do you think you're going to fall in love with me, Dr Anderson?'

She looked at him and the air snapped tight with tension. 'Don't be ridiculous!' Her voice was slightly husky. 'I don't believe in love.'

Could she feel it? Gio wondered. Could she feel what he was feeling?

'Then where is the problem?' He spread lean, bronzed hands and flashed her a smile. 'There is no risk of you falling in love with me. That makes me no more than a lodger.'

But a lodger with a definite interest.

'You don't know what they're like. Every moment of the day there will be little comments. Little asides. They'll drive us mad.'

'Or we could drive them mad. With a little thought and application, this could work in your favour.'

Her glance was suspicious. 'How?'

'Mary and Rita are determined to set you up, no?'

'Yes, but—'

'Clearly they believe that if they put a man under your nose, you will fall in love with him. So—I move in with you and when they see that you have no trouble at all resisting me, they will give up.'

She stared at him thoughtfully. 'You think that will work?'

'Why wouldn't it?'

'You don't know them. They don't give up easily.' The tension had passed and she was suddenly crisp and businesslike. 'And, to be honest, I don't know if I can share a house with someone. I've lived alone since I was eighteen.'

It sounded lonely to him. 'I can assure you that I'm house trained. I'm very clean and I pick up after myself.'

This time there was no answering smile. 'I'm used to having my own space.'

'Me, too,' Gio said smoothly. Was that what the problem was? She liked her independence? 'But Mary said that your house is large…'

'Yes.'

'Then we need hardly see each other.' In truth he'd made up his mind that he'd be seeing plenty of her but decided that the way to achieve that was a step at a time. He was fascinated by Alice Anderson. She was complex. Interesting. Unpredictable. And he knew instinctively that any show of interest on his part would be met with suspicion and rejection. If he looked relaxed and unconcerned about the whole situation, maybe she would, too. 'And think of it this way—' he was suddenly struck by inspiration '—it will give you a chance to brief me fully on the practice, the patients, everything I need to know.'

She looked suddenly thoughtful and he could see her mentally sifting through what he'd just said. 'Yes.' She gave a sharp nod. 'You're right that it will give us plenty of opportunity to talk about work. All right.' She took a deep breath, as if bracing herself. 'Let's lock up here and make a move. Where did you park?'

'At the top of the hill, in the public car park.'

'There are three spaces outside the surgery. You can

use one of those from now on.' She delved into her bag and removed a set of keys. 'I'll give you a lift to your car. Let's go.'

CHAPTER FOUR

STILL fuming about Mary and Rita, Alice jabbed the key into the ignition and gripped the steering-wheel.

She'd been thoroughly outmanoeuvred.

Why had she been foolish enough to let them arrange accommodation? Why hadn't she anticipated that they'd be up to their usual tricks? Because her mind didn't work like theirs, she thought savagely, that was why.

Vowing to tackle the two of them as soon as Gio wasn't around, Alice drove away from the car park, aware that his low black sports car was following close behind her.

Her mind on Mary and Rita, she changed gear with more anger than care and then winced at the hideous crunch. Reminding herself that her car wasn't up to a large degree of abuse, she forced herself to take a calming breath.

They'd set her up yet again, she knew they had. Rita and Mary. The two mother figures in her life. And they'd done it without even bothering to meet the man in question. Somehow they'd both decided that an attractive single guy was going to be perfect for her. It didn't matter that they'd never even met him, that they knew absolutely nothing about him. He was single and she was single and that was all it should take for the magic to kick in.

Anger spurted inside her and Alice thumped the steering-wheel with the heel of her hand and crunched the gears again. They were a pair of interfering old—old…

She really wanted to stay angry but how could she be when she knew that they were only doing it because they cared? When she remembered just how good they'd been to her since her very first day in the practice?

No, better to go along with their little plan and prove to them once and for all that love just didn't work for her. Gio Moretti was right. If she did this, maybe then they'd finally get the message about the way she wanted to live her life.

Yes, that was it. They obviously believed that Gio Moretti was the answer to any woman's prayers. When they realised that he wasn't the answer to hers, maybe they'd leave her alone. She'd live with him if only to prove that she wasn't interested. Since they considered him irresistible, her ability to resist him with no problem should prove something, shouldn't it?

Satisfied with her plan, she gave a swift nod and a smile as she flicked the indicator and took the narrow, winding road that led down to her house.

Her grip on the steering-wheel relaxed slightly. And living with him wouldn't be so bad. Gio seemed like a perfectly civilised guy. He was intelligent and well qualified. His experience in medicine was clearly very different to hers. She would certainly be able to learn from him.

And as for the logistics of the arrangement, she would put him in the guest room at the top of the house that had an *en suite* bathroom so she need never see him. He could come and go without bothering her. They need never have a conversation that didn't involve a patient. And when Mary and Rita saw how things were, they'd surely give up their quest to find her love.

Having satisfied herself that the situation wasn't irredeemable, she stepped on the brake, pulled in to allow another car to pass on the narrow road and drove the last stretch of road that curved down towards the sea.

The crowds of tourists dwindled and immediately she felt calmer.

This was her life. Her world.

The tide was out, the mudflats stretched in front of her and birds swooped and settled on the sandbanks. Behind her were towering cliffs of jagged rock that led out into the sea, and in front of her was the curving mouth of the river, winding lazily inland.

Cornwall.

Home.

Checking that he was still behind her, she touched the brake with her foot, turned right down the tiny track that led down to the water's edge and turned off the engine.

The throaty roar of the sports car behind her died and immediately peace washed over her. For a moment she was tempted to kick her shoes off and walk barefoot, but, as usual, time pressed against her wishes. She had a new lodger to show round and some reading that she needed to finish. And she was going to have to cook something for dinner.

With a shudder of distaste she stepped out of the car feeling hot, sticky and desperate for a cool shower. Wondering when the weather was finally going to break, she turned and watched as Gio slid out of his car and glanced around him. It was a long moment before he spoke.

'This place is amazing.' His hair gleamed glossy dark in the sunlight and the soft fabric of his T-shirt clung to his broad, powerful shoulders. There was a strength about him, an easy confidence that came with maturity, and Alice was suddenly gripped by a shimmer of something unfamiliar.

'Most people consider it to be lonely and isolated. They lecture me on the evils of burying myself somewhere so remote.'

'Do they?' He stood for a moment, legs planted firmly apart in a totally masculine stance, his gaze fixed on the view before him. 'I suppose that's fortunate. If everyone loved it here, it would cease to be so peaceful. You must see some very rare birds.'

'Over fifty different species.' Surprised by the observation, she leaned into her car to retrieve her bag, wondering whether he was genuinely interested in wildlife or whether he was just humouring her. Probably the latter, she decided. The man needed accommodation.

She slammed her car door without bothering to lock it and glanced at his face again. He looked serious enough.

He removed a suitcase from his boot. 'How long have you lived here?'

'Four years.' She delved in her bag for the keys and walked up the path. 'I found this house on my second day here. I was cycling along and there it was. Uninhabited, dilapidated and set apart from everything and everyone.' *Just like her.* She shook off the thought and wriggled the key into the lock. 'It took me a year to do it up sufficiently to live in it, another two years to get it to the state it's in now.'

He removed his sunglasses and glanced at her in surprise. 'You did the work yourself?'

She caught the look and smiled. 'Never judge by appearances, Dr Moretti. I have hidden muscles.' She pushed open the front door and stooped to pick up the post. 'I'll show you where you're sleeping and then meet you in the kitchen. I can fill you in on everything you need to know while we eat.'

She deposited the post, unopened, on the hall table and made a mental note to water the plants before she went to bed.

'It's beautiful.' His eyes scanned the wooden floors, which she'd sanded herself and then painted white, lifted to the filmy white curtains that framed large, picture windows and took in the touches of blue in the cushions and the artwork on the walls. He stepped forward to take a closer look at a large watercolour she had displayed in the hall. 'It's good. It has real passion. You can feel the power of the sea.' He frowned at the signature and turned to look at her. 'You paint?'

'Not any more.' She strode towards the stairs, eager to end the conversation. It was becoming too personal and she was always careful to avoid the personal. 'No time. Your room is at the top of the house and it has its own bathroom. It should be perfectly possible for us to lead totally separate lives.'

She said it to reassure herself as much to remind him and took the stairs two at a time and flung open a door. 'Here we are. You should be comfortable enough here and, anyway, it's only short term.' She broke off and he gave a smile.

'Of course.'

'Look, I don't mean to be rude and I'm thrilled that you're going to be working here, but I'm just not that great at sharing my living space with anyone, OK?' She shrugged awkwardly, wondering why she felt the need to explain herself. 'I'm selfish. I'm the first to admit it. I've lived on my own for too long to be anything else.'

And it was the way she preferred it. It was just a shame that Rita and Mary couldn't get the message.

He strode over to the huge windows and stared at the view. 'You're not being rude. If I lived here, I'd protect it, too.' He turned to face her. 'And I'm not intending to invade your personal space, Alice. You can relax.'

Relax?

His rich accent turned her name into something exotic and exciting and she gave a slight shiver. There would be no relaxing while he was staying with her.

'Then we won't have a problem.' She backed towards the door. 'Make yourself at home. I'm going to take a shower and change. Come down when you're ready. I'll be in the kitchen. Making supper.'

Her least favourite pastime. She gave a sigh of irritation as she left the room. She considered both cooking and eating to be a monumental waste of time but, with a guest in the house, she could hardly suggest that they skip a meal in favour of a bowl of cereal, which was her usual standby when she couldn't be bothered to cook.

Which meant opening the fridge and creating something out of virtually nothing. She just hoped that Gio Moretti wasn't too discerning when it came to his palate.

Her blue eyes narrowed and she gave a soft smile as she pushed open the door to her own bedroom and made for the shower, stripping off clothes as she walked and flinging them on the bed.

If the way to a man's heart was through his stomach, she was surprised that Mary and Rita had given their plan even the remotest chance of success.

It didn't take a genius to know that it was going to be hard for a man to harbour romantic notions about a woman who had just poisoned him.

When Gio strolled into the kitchen after a shower and a shave, she was grating cheese into a bowl with no apparent signs of either skill or enthusiasm. He watched with amusement and no small degree of interest and wondered who had designed the kitchen.

It was a cook's paradise. White slatted units and lots of glass reflected the light and a huge stainless-steel oven gleamed and winked, its spotless surface suggesting it had never been used. In fact, the whole kitchen looked as though it belonged in a show home and it took him less than five seconds of watching the usually competent Alice wrestle with a lump of cheese to understand why.

At the far end of the room French doors opened onto the pretty garden. Directly in front of the doors, positioned to make the most of the view, was a table covered in medical magazines, a few textbooks and several sheets of paper covered in neat handwriting.

He could picture her there, her face serious as she read her way through all the academic medical journals, checking the facts. He'd seen enough to know that Alice

Anderson was comfortable with facts. Possibly more comfortable with facts than she was with people.

He wondered why.

In his experience, there was usually a reason for the way people chose to live their lives.

'Cheese on toast all right with you?' She turned, still grating, her eyes fixed on his face. 'Oh…'

'Something is wrong?'

She blew a wisp of blonde hair out of her eyes. 'You look…different.'

He smiled and strolled towards her. 'More like a doctor?'

'Maybe. Ow.' She winced as the grater grazed her knuckles and adjusted her grip. 'I wasn't expecting guests, I'm afraid, so I haven't shopped. And I have to confess that I loathe cooking.' Her blonde hair was still damp from the shower and she'd changed into a pair of linen trousers and a pink top. She looked young and feminine and a long way from the brisk, competent professional he'd met earlier. The kitchen obviously flustered her and he found her slightly clumsy approach to cooking surprisingly appealing. In fact, he was fast discovering that there were many parts of Alice Anderson that he found appealing.

'Anything I can do?' Wondering if he should take over or whether that would damage her ego, he strolled over to her, lifted a piece of cheese and sniffed it. 'What is it?'

'The cheese?' She turned on the grill and watched for a moment as if not entirely confident that it would work. 'Goodness knows. The sort that comes wrapped in tight plastic. Cheddar or something, I suppose. Why?'

He tried not to wince at the vision of cheese tightly

wrapped in plastic. 'I'm Italian. We happen to love cheese. Mozzarella, fontina, ricotta, marscapone…'

'This is just something I grabbed from the supermarket a few weeks ago. It was covered with blue bits but I chopped them off. I assumed they weren't supposed to be there. I don't think they were there when I bought it.' She dropped the grater and stared down at the pile of cheese with a distinct lack of enthusiasm. 'There should be some salad in the fridge, if you're interested.'

He opened her fridge and stared. It was virtually empty. Making a mental note to shop at the earliest convenient moment, he reached for a limp, sorry piece of lettuce and examined it thoughtfully. 'I'm not bothered about salad,' he murmured, and she glanced up, her face pink from the heat of the grill, her teeth gritted.

'Fine. Whatever. This is nearly ready.' She pulled out the grill pan and fanned her hand over the contents to stop it smoking. 'I'm not that great a cook but at least it's food, and that's all that matters. Good job I'm not really trying to seduce you, Dr Moretti.' She flashed him a wicked smile as she slid the contents of the grill pan onto two plates. 'If the way to a man's heart is through his stomach, I'm completely safe.'

She wasn't joking about her culinary skills. Gio stared down at the burnt edges of the toast and the patchy mix of melted and unmelted cheese and suddenly realised why she was so slim. It was a good job he was starving and willing to eat virtually anything. Suddenly he understood Mary's suggestion that they get a takeaway. 'Did you eat lunch today?'

She fished knives and forks out of a drawer and sat down at the table, pushing aside the piles of journals and books to make room for the plates. 'I can't remember. I might have had something at some point. So what's your opinion on Harriet?' She pushed cutlery across the table and poured some water. 'Do you think she is depressed?'

He wondered if she even realised that she was talking about work again.

Did she do it on purpose to avoid a conversation of a more personal nature?

He picked up a fork and tried to summon up some enthusiasm for the meal ahead. It was a challenge. For him a meal was supposed to be a total experience. An event. A time to indulge the palate and the senses simultaneously. Clearly, for Alice it was just a means of satisfying the gnawing in her stomach.

Glancing down at his plate, he wondered whether he was going to survive the experience of Alice's cooking or whether he was going to require medical attention.

She definitely needed educating about food.

'Is Harriet depressed? It's possible. I'll certainly follow it up.' He cautiously tasted the burnt offering on his plate and decided that it was the most unappetizing meal he'd eaten for a long time. 'Postnatal depression is a serious condition.'

'And often missed. She was fine after the twins but that's not necessarily significant, of course.' Alice finished her toasted cheese with brisk efficiency and no visible signs of enjoyment and put down her fork with an apologetic glance in his direction. 'Sorry to eat so quickly. I was starving. I don't think I managed to eat at all yesterday.'

'Are you serious?'

'Perfectly. We had a bit of a drama in the bay. The

lifeboat was called out to two children who'd managed to drift out to sea in their inflatable boat.' She broke off and sipped her drink. 'I spent my lunch-hour over with the crew, making sure they were all right. By the time I finished I had a queue of people in the surgery. I forgot to eat.'

To Gio, who had never forgotten to eat in his life, such a situation was incomprehensible. 'You need to seriously rethink your lifestyle.'

'You sound like Mary and Rita. I happen to like my lifestyle. It works for me.' With a fatalistic shrug she finished her water and stood up. 'So, Dr Moretti, what can I tell you about the practice to make your life easier? At this time of year we see a lot of tourists with the usual sorts of problems. Obviously, on top of the locals, it makes us busy, as you discovered today.'

All she thought about was work, he reflected, watching as she lifted a medical journal from the pile on the table and absently scanned the contents. She was driven. Obsessed. 'Do you do a minor accident clinic?'

'No.' She shook her head and dropped the journal back on the pile. 'David and I tried it two years ago but, to be honest, there were days when we were swamped and days when we were sitting around. We decided it was better just to fit them into surgery time. We have a very good relationship with the coastguard and the local paramedics. Sometimes they call on us, sometimes we call on them. We also have a good relationship with the local police.'

'The police?' His attention was caught by the gentle sway of her hips as she walked across the kitchen. Her movements were graceful and utterly feminine and from nowhere he felt a sharp tug of lust.

Gritting his teeth, he tried to talk sense into himself. *They were colleagues.*

He'd known her for less than a day.

'Beach parties.' She lifted the kettle and filled it. 'At this time of year we have a lot of teenagers just hanging out on the beach. Usually the problem's just too much alcohol, as you saw this morning. Sometimes it's drugs.'

To hide the fact that he was studying her, Gio glanced out towards the sea and tried to imagine it crowded with hordes of teenagers. *Tried to drag his mind away from the tempting curve of her hips.* 'Looks peaceful to me. It's hard to imagine it otherwise.'

She rested those same hips against the work surface while she waited for the kettle to boil. 'They don't come down this far. They congregate on the beach beyond the harbour. The surf is good. Too good sometimes, and then we get a fair few surfing accidents, as you also noticed this morning. Coffee?'

Gio opened his mouth to say yes and then winced as he saw her reaching into a cupboard for a jar. 'You are using instant coffee?'

She pulled a face. 'I know. It's not my favourite either, but it's better than nothing and I've run out of fresh. One of the drawbacks of living out here is that both the supermarket and the nearest espresso machine are a car ride away.'

'Not any more.'

'Don't tell me.' She spooned coffee into a mug. 'You've brought your own espresso machine.'

'Of course. It was a key part of my luggage. Along with a large supply of the very best beans.'

She stilled, the spoon still in her hand. 'You're not serious?'

'Coffee is extremely serious,' he said dryly. 'If you expect me to work hard, I need my daily fix, and if today is anything to go by then I'm not going to have time to pop up the hill to that excellent bakery.'

She scooped her hair away from her face and there was longing in her eyes. 'You're planning to make fresh coffee every morning?'

'*Si.*' He wondered why she was even asking the question when it seemed entirely normal to him. 'It is the only way I can get through the day.'

The smile spread across her face. 'Now, if Mary had mentioned that, I would have cancelled your flat with the letting agent myself.' She licked her lips, put down the spoon, a hunger in her eyes. 'Does your fancy machine make enough for two cups?'

He decided that if it guaranteed him one of her smiles, he'd stand over the machine all morning. 'A decent cup of coffee to start your day will be part of my fee for invading your space,' he offered. Along with the cooking, but he decided to wait a while before breaking that to her in case she was offended. 'So tell me about Rita and Mary.' He wanted to know about their relationship with her. Why they felt the need to set her up.

He wanted to know everything there was to know about Alice Anderson.

'They've worked in the practice for ever. Twenty-five years at least. Can you imagine that?' She shook her head. 'It helps, of course, because they know everything about everyone. History is important, don't you think, Dr Moretti?'

He wondered about her history. He wondered what had made a beautiful woman like her choose to bury herself in her work and live apart from others. It felt wrong. Not the setting, he mused as he glanced out of the window. The setting was perfect. But in his opinion it was a setting designed to be shared with someone special.

Realising that she was waiting for an answer, he smiled, amused by her earnest expression. She was delightfully serious. 'I can see that history is important in general practice.'

'It gives you clues. Not knowing a patient's history is often like trying to solve a murder with no access to clues.' Her eyes narrowed. 'I suppose as a surgeon, it's different. It's more task orientated. You get the patient on the operating table and you solve the problem.'

'Not necessarily that simple.' He sat back in his chair, comfortable in her kitchen. *In her company.* The problems of the past year faded. 'In plastic surgery the patient's wishes, hopes, dreams are all an important part of the picture. Appearance can affect people's lives. As a society, we're shallow. We see and we judge. As a surgeon you have to take that into account. You need to understand what's needed and decided whether you can deliver.'

'You did face lifts? Nose jobs?'

He smiled. It was a common misconception and it didn't offend him. 'That wasn't my field of speciality,' he said quietly. 'I did paediatrics. Cleft palates, hare lips. In between running my clinic in Milan, I did volunteer work in developing countries. Children with unrepaired clefts lead very isolated lives. Often they can't go to school—they're ostracised from the community, no chance of employment...'

She was staring at him, a frown in her blue eyes as if she was reassessing him. 'I had no idea.' She picked up her coffee, but her focus was on him, not the mug in her hand. 'That's so interesting. And tough.'

'Tough, rewarding, frustrating.' He gave a shrug. 'All those things. Like every branch of medicine, I suppose. I also did a lot of training. Showing local doctors new techniques.' He waited for the dull ache of disappointment that always came when he was talking about the past, but there was nothing. Instead he felt more relaxed than he could ever recall feeling.

'It must have been hard for you to give it up.'

He shrugged and felt a twinge in his shoulder. 'Life sometimes forces change on us but sometimes it's a change we should have made ourselves if we only had the courage. I was ready for a change.'

He sensed that she was going to ask him more, delve deeper, and then she seemed to withdraw.

'Well, there's certainly variety in our practice. If you're good with babies, you can run the baby clinic. David used to do it.'

She was talking about work again, he mused. 'Immunisations, I assume?' Always, she avoided the personal. *Was she afraid of intimacy?*

'That and other things.' She sipped at her coffee. 'It's a really busy clinic. We expanded its remit a few months ago to encourage mothers to see us with their problems during the clinic rather than making appointments during normal surgery hours. It means that they don't have to make separate appointments for themselves and we reduce the number of toddlers running around the waiting room.' Her fingers tightened on the mug. 'I have to confess it isn't my forte.'

'I've seen enough of your work to know that you're an excellent doctor.' He watched as the colour touched her cheekbones.

'Oh, I can do the practical stuff.' She gave a shrug and turned her back on him, dumping her mug in the sink. 'It's everything that goes with it that I can't handle. All the emotional stuff. I'm terrible at that. How are you with worried mothers, Dr Moretti?' She turned and her blonde hair swung gently round her head.

Was she afraid of other people's emotions or her own? Pondering the question, he flashed her a wicked smile. 'Worried women are my speciality, Dr Anderson.'

She threw back her head and laughed. 'I'll just bet they are, Dr Moretti. I'll just bet they are.'

Alice woke to the delicious smells of freshly ground coffee, rolled over and then remembered Gio Moretti. Living here. In her house.

She sat upright, pushed the heavy cloud of sleep away and checked the clock. 6 a.m. He was obviously an early riser, like her.

Tempted by the smell and the prospect of a good cup of coffee to start her day, she padded into the shower, dressed quickly and followed her nose.

She pushed open the kitchen door, her mind automatically turning to work, and then stopped dead, taken aback by the sight of Gio half-naked in her kitchen.

'Oh!' She'd assumed he was up and dressed, instead of which he was wearing jeans again. This time with nothing else. His chest was bare and the muscles of his shoulders flexed as he reached for the coffee.

He was gorgeous.

The thought stopped her dead and she frowned, surprised at herself for noticing and more than a little irritated. And then she gave a dismissive shrug. So what? Despite what Rita and Mary obviously thought, she was neither blind nor brain dead. And it wasn't as if she hadn't experienced sexual attraction before. She had. The important thing was not to mistake it for 'love'.

He turned to reach for a cup and she saw the harsh, jagged scars running down his back. 'That looks painful.'

The minute she said the words she wished she hadn't. Was he sensitive about it? Perhaps she wasn't supposed to mention it. If he was the type of guy that spent all day staring in the mirror, then perhaps it bothered him.

'Not as painful as it used to. *Buongiorno.*' He flashed her a smile and handed her a cup, totally at ease in her kitchen. 'I wasn't expecting you up this early. I have to have coffee before I can face the shower.'

'I know the feeling.' Wondering how he got the scar, she took the cup with a nod of thanks and wandered over to the table, trying not to look in his direction.

She might not believe in love but she could see when a man was attractive and Gio Moretti was certainly attractive. When she'd said he could have her spare room, she hadn't imagined he'd be walking around her house half-naked. It was unsettling and more than a little distracting.

She sat down. Her body suddenly felt hot and uncomfortable and she slid a finger around the neck of her shirt and glanced at the sun outside. 'It's going to be another scorcher today.' Even though she made a point of not looking in his direction, she sensed his gaze on her.

'You're feeling hot, Alice?'

Something in his voice made her turn her head. Her eyes met hers and an unexpected jolt shook her body. 'It's warm in here, yes.' She caught her breath, broke the eye contact and picked up her coffee, but not before her brain had retained a clear image of a bronzed, muscular chest covered in curling dark hairs. He was all muscle and masculinity and her throat felt suddenly dry. She took a sip of coffee. 'This is delicious. Thank you.'

Still holding her cup, she stared out of the window and tried to erase the memory of his half-naked body. She wasn't used to having a man in her kitchen. It was all too informal. Too intimate.

Everything she avoided.

To take her mind off the problem she did what she always did. She thought about work.

'Rita has a baby clinic this afternoon,' she said brightly, watching as a heron rose from the smooth calm of the estuary that led to sea and flew off with a graceful sweep of its wings. 'Invariably she manages it by herself but sometimes she needs one of us to—'

'Alice, *cara.*' His voice came from behind her, deep and heavily accented. 'I need at least two cups of coffee before I can even think about work, let alone talk about it.' His hands came up and touched her shoulders and she stiffened. She wasn't used to being touched. No one touched her.

'I just thought you should know that—'

'This kitchen has the most beautiful view.' He kept his hands on her shoulders, his touch light and relaxed. 'Enjoy it. It's still early. Leave thoughts of work until later. Look at the mist. Enjoy the silence. It's perfect.'

She sat still, heart pounding, thoroughly unsettled. Usually her kitchen soothed her. Calmed her. But today she could feel the little spurts of tension darting through her shoulders.

It was just having someone else in the house, she told herself. Inevitably it altered her routine.

Abandoning her plan to read some journals while drinking her coffee as she usually did, she stood up and firmly extricated herself from his hold.

'I need to get going.' Annoyed with herself and even more annoyed with him, she walked across the room, taking her cup with her. 'I'll meet you at the surgery later.'

His eyes flickered to the clock on the wall. 'Alice, it's only 6.30.' His voice was a soft, accented drawl. 'And you haven't finished your coffee.'

'There's masses of paperwork to plough through.' She drank the coffee quickly and put the cup on the nearest worktop. 'Thank you. A great improvement on instant.'

His eyes were locked on her face. 'You haven't had breakfast.'

'I don't need breakfast.' What she needed most of all was space. Air to breathe. The safety of her usual routine. She backed out of the door, needing to escape. 'I'll see you later.'

Grabbing her bag and her jacket, she strode out of the house, fumbling for her keys as she let the door swing shut behind her.

Oh, bother and blast.

Instead of starting her day in a calm, organised frame

of mind, as she usually did, she felt unsettled and on edge and the reason why was perfectly obvious.

She didn't need a lodger and she certainly didn't need a lodger that she noticed, she thought to herself as she slid into the sanctuary of her car.

And she was *definitely* going to kill Mary when she saw her.

He made her nervous.

She claimed not to believe in love and yet there was chemistry between them. An elemental attraction that he'd felt from the first moment. And it was growing stronger by the minute.

Gio made himself a second cup of coffee and drank it seated at the little table overlooking the garden and the sea.

She was serious, academic and obviously totally un-accustomed to having a man in her life. He'd felt the sudden tension in her shoulders when he'd touched her. Felt her discomfort and her sudden anxiety.

He frowned and stretched his legs out in front of him.

In his family, touching was part of life. Everyone touched. Hugged. Held. It was what they did. But not everyone was the same, of course.

And, for whatever reason, he sensed that Alice wasn't used to being touched. *Wasn't comfortable being touched.*

The English were generally more reserved and emo-tionally distant, of course, so it could be that. He drained his coffee-cup. Or it could be something else. Some-thing linked with the reason he was sitting here now instead of in a flat in another part of town.

Why had Mary seen the need to interfere?

Why did she think that Alice needed help finding a man in her life?

And, given his distaste for matchmaking attempts, why wasn't he running fast in the opposite direction?

Why did he suddenly feel comfortable and content?

The question didn't need much answering. Everything about Alice intrigued him. She was complex and unpredictable. She had a beautiful smile but it only appeared after a significant amount of coaxing. She was clever and clearly caring and yet she herself had humbly confessed that she wasn't good with emotions.

And she was uncomfortable with being touched.

Which was a shame, he thought to himself as he finished his coffee. Because he'd made up his mind that he was going to be touching her a lot. So she was going to have to start getting used to it.

CHAPTER FIVE

MARY sailed into the surgery just as Alice scooped the post from the mat. 'You're early.' There was disappointment in her expression, as if she'd expected something different. 'So—did you have a lovely evening?'

'Wonderful. Truly wonderful.' Alice dropped the post onto the reception desk to be sorted and gave a wistful sigh, deriving wicked satisfaction from the look of hope that lit Mary's face. 'I must do it more often.'

'Do what more often?'

'Go home early, of course.' Alice smiled sweetly. 'I caught up on so many things.'

Mary's shoulders sagged. 'Caught up on what? How was your lodger?'

'Who?' Alice adopted a blank expression and then waved a hand vaguely. 'Oh, you mean Dr Moretti? Fine, I think. I wouldn't really know. I hardly saw him.'

Mary dropped her bag with a thump and a scowl. 'You didn't spend the evening together?'

'Not at all. Why would we? He's my lodger, not my date.' Alice leaned forward and picked up the contents of her in tray. 'But he does make tremendous coffee. I suppose I have you to thank for that, given that you arranged it all.'

'You already drink too much coffee,' Mary scolded as they both walked towards the consulting rooms. She caught Alice's arm in a firm grip. 'Are you serious? You didn't spend any time with him at all?'

Alice shrugged her off. 'None.'

'If that's true, you're a sad case.' Her eyes narrowed. 'You're teasing me, aren't you?'

'All right, I'll tell you the truth.' Thoroughly enjoying herself now, Alice threw Mary a saucy wink as she pushed open the door to her room. 'I'm grateful to you, really I am. Even I can see that Gio Moretti is handsome. I don't suppose they come much handsomer. If I have to share my house with someone I'd so much rather it was someone decorative. I could hardly concentrate on my breakfast this morning because he was standing in my kitchen half-naked. *What* a body!' She gave an exaggerated sigh and pressed her palm against her heart. 'I'd have to be a fool not to be interested in a man like him, wouldn't you agree?'

'Alice—'

'And I'm certainly not a fool.' She dropped her bag behind her desk. 'Anyway, I just want you to know that we've been at it all night like rabbits and now I've definitely got him out of my system so you can safely find him somewhere else to live, you interfering old—'

'*Buongiorno.*'

The deep voice came from the doorway and Alice whirled round, her face turning pink with embarrassment. She caught the wicked humour in his dark eyes and cursed inwardly.

Why had he chosen that precise moment to walk down the corridor?

He lounged in her doorway, dressed in tailored trousers and a crisp cotton shirt that looked both expensive and stylish. The sleeves were rolled up to his elbows, revealing bronzed forearms dusted with dark hairs. The laughter in his eyes told her that he'd heard every word. 'You left without breakfast, Dr Anderson. And after such a long, taxing night…' He lingered over each syllable, his rich, Italian accent turning the words into something decadent and sinful '…you need to replenish your energy levels.'

Mary glanced between them, her expression lifting, and Alice suppressed a groan. Friendly banter. Teasing. All designed to give Mary totally the wrong idea. And she'd been the one to start it.

'Finally, someone else to scold you about not eating proper meals.' Mary put her hands on her hips and gave a satisfied nod. 'If Dr Moretti values his stomach lining, he'll take over the cooking.'

'I'm perfectly capable of cooking,' Alice snapped, sitting down at her desk and switching on her computer with a stab of her finger. 'It's just that I don't enjoy it very much and I have so many other more important things to do with my time.'

'Like work.' Mary looked at Gio. 'While you're at it, you might want to reform her on that count, too.' She walked out of the room, leaving Alice glaring after her.

'I've decided that David had the right idea after all. London is looking better all the time. In London, no one cares what the person next to them is doing. No one cares whether they eat breakfast, work or don't work.

And for sure, no one cares about the state of anyone else's love life.' She hit the return key on the keyboard with more force than was necessary, aware that Gio was watching her, a thoughtful expression in his dark eyes. His shoulders were still against the doorframe and he didn't seem in any hurry to go anywhere.

'She really cares about you.'

Alice stilled. He was right, of course. Mary did care about her. And she'd never had that before. Until she'd arrived in Smuggler's Cove, she'd never experienced interference as a result of caring.

'I know she does.' Alice bit her lip. 'I wish I could convince her that I'm fine on my own. That this is what I want. How I want to live my life.'

His gaze was steady. 'Sounds lonely to me, Dr Anderson. And perhaps a bit cowardly.'

'Cowardly?' She forgot about her computer and sat back in her chair, more than a little outraged. 'What's that supposed to mean?'

He walked further into the room, his eyes fixed on her face. 'People who avoid relationships are usually afraid of getting hurt.'

'Or perhaps they're just particularly well adjusted and evolved,' Alice returned sweetly. 'This is the twenty-first century and we no longer all believe that a man is necessary to validate and enhance our lives.'

'Is that so?' His gaze dropped to her mouth and she felt her heart stumble and kick in her chest.

With a frown of irritation she turned her head and concentrated on her computer screen. Why was he looking at her like that? Studying her? As if he was trying to see deep inside her mind? Her fingers drummed a rhythm on the desk. Well, that was a part of herself that she kept private. Like all the other parts.

She looked up, her expression cool and discouraging. 'We don't all have to agree on everything, Dr Moretti. Our differences are what make the world an interesting place to live. And now I'm sure you have patients to see and I know that I certainly do.' To make her point, she reached across her desk and pressed the buzzer to alert her first patient. 'Oh, and please don't give Mary and Rita the impression that we're living a cosy life together. They'll be unbearable.'

'But surely the point is to prove that we can be cosy and yet you can still resist me,' he reminded her in silky tones, and she stared at him, speechless. 'Isn't that the message you want them to receive? Unless, of course, you are having trouble resisting me.'

'Oh, please!' She gave an exclamation of impatience and looked up just as the patient knocked on the door. 'Let's just move on.'

'Yes, let's do that.' He kept his hand on the doorhandle, his eyes glinting darkly, 'but at least try and keep this authentic. For the record, you would not get me out of your system in one night, *cara mia*.'

Her mouth fell open and she searched in vain for a witty reply. And failed.

His smile widened and he wandered out of the room, leaving her fuming.

Alice took refuge in work and fortunately there was plenty of it.

Her first patient was a woman who was worried about a rash on her daughter's mouth.

'She had this itchy, red sore and then suddenly it turned into a blister and it's been oozing.' The mother pulled a face and hugged the child. 'Poor thing. It's really bothering her.'

Alice took one look at the thick, honey-coloured crust that had formed over the lesion and made an instant diagnosis. *Impetigo contagiosa,* she decided, caused by *Staphyloccocus aureus* and possibly group A beta-haemolytic streptococcus. This was one of the things she loved about medicine, she thought as she finished her examination and felt a rush of satisfaction. You were given clues. Signs. And you had to interpret them. Behind everything was a cause. It was just a question of finding it.

In this case she had no doubt. 'She has impetigo, Mrs Wood.' She turned back to her computer, selected a drug and pressed the print key. 'It's a very common skin condition, particularly in children. As it's only in one area I'm going to give you some cream to apply to the affected area. You need to wash the skin several times a day and remove the crusts. Then apply the cream. But make sure you wash your hands carefully because it's highly contagious.'

'Can she go back to nursery?'

Alice shook her head. 'Not until the lesions are cleared. Make sure you don't share towels.'

Mrs Wood sighed. 'That's more holiday I'll have to take, then. Being a working mother is a nightmare. I wonder why I bother sometimes.'

'It must be difficult.' Alice took the prescription from the printer and signed it. 'Here we are. Come back in a week if it isn't better.'

Mrs Wood left the room clutching her prescription and Alice moved on to the next patient. And the next.

She was reading a discharge letter from a surgeon when her door opened and Gio walked in, juggling two coffees and a large paper bag.

'I'm fulfilling my brief from Mary. Breakfast.' He flashed her a smile, kicked the door shut with his foot and placed everything on the desk in front of her. He ripped open the bag and waved a hand. 'Help yourself.'

She sat back in her chair and stared at him in exasperation. She never stopped for a break when she was seeing patients. It threw her concentration and just meant an even longer day. 'I've still got patients to see.'

'Actually, you haven't. At least, not at this exact moment. I checked with Mary.' He sat down in the chair next to her desk. 'Your last patient has cancelled so you've got a break. And so have I. Let's make the most of it.'

She stared at the selection of croissants and muffins. 'I'm not really hungry but now you're here we could quickly run through the referral strategy for—'

'Alice.' He leaned forward, a flash of humour in his dark eyes. 'If you're about to mention work, hold the thought.' He pushed the bag towards her. 'I refuse to discuss anything until I've seen you eat.'

The scent of warm, freshly baked cakes wafted under her nose. 'But I—'

'Didn't eat breakfast,' he reminded her calmly, 'and you've got the whole morning ahead of you. You can't get through that workload on one cup of black coffee, even though it was excellent.'

She sighed and her hand hovered over the bag. Eventually her fingers closed over a muffin. 'Fine. Thanks. If I eat this, will you leave me alone?'

'Possibly.' He waited until she'd taken a bite. 'Now we can talk about work. I'm interested in following up on Harriet. You mentioned that there's a baby clinic this afternoon. Is she likely to attend?'

'Possibly.' The muffin was still warm and tasted delicious. She wondered how she could have thought she wasn't hungry. She was starving. 'Rita would know whether she's down for immunisation. Or she may just come to have the baby weighed. Gina is around this morning, too. It would be worth talking to her. I've got a meeting with her at eleven-fifteen, to talk about our MMR rates.'

'I'll join you. Then I can discuss Harriet.'

'Fine.' Her gaze slid longingly at the remaining muffins. 'Can I have another?'

'Eat.' He pushed them towards her and she gave a guilty smile.

'I'll cook supper tonight in return.' She thought she saw a look of alarm cross his face but then decided she must have imagined it.

'There's no need, I thought we could—'

'I insist.' It was the least she could do, she thought, devouring the muffin and reached for another without even thinking. She loathed cooking, but there were times when it couldn't be avoided. 'Last night's supper of cheese on toast was hardly a gourmet treat. Tonight I'll do a curry.' She'd made one once before and it hadn't turned out too badly.

'Alice, why don't you let me—' He broke off and turned as the door opened and Rita walked in.

'Can you come to the waiting room? Betty needs advice.'

Alice brushed the crumbs from her lap and stood up. 'I'll come now. Nice breakfast. Thanks.'

Dropping the empty bag in the bin on his way past, Gio followed, wondering if she even realised that she'd eaten her way through three muffins.

It was almost eleven o'clock, and she'd been up since dawn and working on an empty stomach until he'd intervened.

Something definitely needed to be done about her lifestyle.

He gave a wry smile. Even more so if he was going to be living with her. After sampling her cheese on toast, he didn't dare imagine what her curry would be like, but he had a suspicion that the after-effects might require medication.

He walked into the reception area and watched while she walked over to the couple standing at the desk.

'Betty? What's happened?'

'Eating too quickly, that's what happened.' Betty scowled at her husband but there was worry in her eyes. 'Thought I'd cook him a nice bit of fish for breakfast, straight from the quay, but he wasn't looking what he was doing and now he's got a bone lodged in his throat. And, of course, it has to be right at peak season when the shop's clogged with people spending money and I can't trust that dizzy girl on her own behind the counter. If we have to go to A and E it will be hours and—'

'Betty.'

Gio watched, fascinated, as Alice put a hand on the woman's arm and interrupted her gently, her voice

steady and confident. 'Calm down. I'm sure we'll
manage to take the bone out here, but if not—' She
broke off as the door opened again and another
woman hurried in, her face disturbingly pale, a hand
resting on her swollen stomach. 'Cathy? Has something happened?'

'Oh, Dr Anderson, I've had the most awful pains this
morning. Ever since I hung out the washing. I didn't
know whether I should just drive straight to the hospital
but Mick has an interview later this morning and I didn't
want to drag him there on a wild-goose chase. I know
surgery has finished, but have you got a minute?'

Obviously not for both at the same time, Gio reflected with something close to amusement. No wonder
Alice looked tired. She never stopped working. Surgery
was finished and still the patients were crowding in. Had
he really thought that he was in for a quiet summer?

He glanced towards the door, half expecting someone
else to appear, but there was no one. 'Point me in the
direction of a pair of Tilley's forceps and I'll deal with
the fishbone,' he said calmly, and Alice gave a brief
nod, her eyes lingering on Cathy's pale face.

'In your consulting room. Forceps are in the top
cupboard above the sink. Thanks.'

Her lack of hesitation impressed him. She might be
a workaholic but at least she didn't have trouble dele-
gating, Gio mused as he introduced himself to the
couple and ushered them into the consulting room.

'If you'll have a seat, Mr…?' He lifted an eyebrow
and the woman gave a stiff smile.

'Norman. Giles and Betty Norman.' Her tone was
crisp and more than a little chilly, but he smiled easily.

'You'll have to forgive me for not knowing who you are. This is only my second day here.'

Betty Norman gave a sniff. 'We run the newsagent across the harbour. If you were local, you'd know that. There have been Normans running the newsagent for five generations.' She looked at him suspiciously, her gaze bordering on the unfriendly. 'That's a foreign accent I'm hearing and you certainly don't look English.'

'That's because I'm Italian.' Gio adjusted the angle of the light. 'And I may be new to the village, Mrs Norman, but I'm not new to medicine so you need have no worries on that score.' He opened a cupboard and selected the equipment he was going to need. 'Mr Norman, I just need to shine a light in your mouth so that I can take a better look at the back of your throat.'

Betty dropped her handbag and folded her arms. 'Well, I just hope you can manage to get the wretched thing out. Some surgeries insist you go to A and E for something like this but we have a business to run. A and E is a sixty-minute round trip at the best of times and then there's the waiting. Dr Anderson is good at this sort of thing. Perhaps we ought to wait until she's finished with young Cathy.'

Aware that he was being tested, Gio bit back a smile, not remotely offended. 'I don't think that's a trip you're going to be making today, Mrs Norman,' he said smoothly, raising his head briefly from his examination to acknowledge her concerns. 'And I don't think you need to wait to see Dr Anderson. I can understand that you're wary of a new doctor but I can assure you that I'm more than up to the job. Why don't you let me try and then we'll see what happens?'

She stared at him, her shoulders tense and unyielding, her mouth pursed in readiness to voice further disapproval, and then he smiled at her and the tension seemed to ooze out of her and her mouth relaxed slightly into a smile of her own.

'Stupid of me to cook fish for breakfast,' she muttered weakly, and Gio returned to his examination.

'Cooking is never stupid, Mrs Norman,' he murmured as he depressed her husband's tongue to enable him to visualise the tonsil. 'And fish is the food of the gods, especially when it's eaten fresh from the sea. I see the bone quite clearly. Removing it should present no difficulty whatsoever.'

He reached for the forceps, adjusted the light and removed the fishbone with such speed and skill that his patient barely coughed.

'There.' He placed the offending bone on a piece of gauze. 'There's the culprit. The back of your throat has been slightly scratched, Mr Norman, so I'm going to give you an antibiotic and ask you to come back in a day for me to just check your throat. If necessary I will refer you to the ENT team at the hospital, but I don't think it will come to that.'

Mr Norman stared at the bone and glanced at his wife, an expression of relief on his face.

'Well—thank goodness.'

She picked up her handbag, all her icy reserve melted away. 'Thank the doctor, not goodness.' She gave Gio a nod of approval. 'Welcome to Smuggler's Cove. I think you're going to fit in well.'

'Thank you.' He smiled, his mind on Alice and her soft mouth. 'I think so, too.'

* * *

Alice watched from the doorway, clocked the killer smile, the Latin charm, and noted Betty's response with a sigh of relief and a flicker of exasperation. Why was it that the members of her sex were so predictable?

She'd briefly examined Cathy and what she'd seen had been enough to convince her that a trip to hospital was necessary for a more detailed check-up. Then she'd returned to the consulting room, prepared to help Gio, only to find that her help clearly wasn't required.

Not only had he removed the fishbone, which she knew could often be a tricky procedure, but had obviously succeeded in winning over the most difficult character in the village.

It amused her that even Betty Norman wasn't immune to a handsome Italian with a sexy smile and for a moment she found herself remembering David's comment about women going weak at the knees. Then she allowed herself a smile. *Not every woman.* Her knees were still functioning as expected, despite Mary's interference.

She could see he was handsome, and she was still walking with no problem.

Clearing her throat, she walked into the room. 'Everything OK?'

But she could see that everything was more than OK. Betty had melted like Cornish ice cream left out in the midday sun.

'Everything is fine.' Betty glanced at her watch, all smiles now. She patted her hair and straightened her blouse. 'I can be back behind the counter before that girl has a chance to make a mistake. Nice meeting you Dr…I didn't catch your name.'

'Moretti.' He extended a lean, bronzed hand. 'Gio Moretti.'

His voice was a warm, accented drawl and Betty flushed a deep shade of pink as she shook his hand. 'Well, thank you again. And welcome. If you need any help with anything, just call into the newsagent's.' She waved a hand, flustered now. 'I'd be more than happy to advise you on anything local.'

Gio smiled. 'I'll remember that.'

'By the way…' She turned to Alice. 'Edith doesn't seem herself at the moment. I can't put my finger on it but something isn't right. It may be nothing, but I thought you should know, given what happened to her last month.'

'I'll check on her.' Alice frowned. 'You think she might have fallen again?'

'That's what's worrying me.' Betty reached for her handbag. 'Iris Leek at number thirty-six has a key if you need to let yourself in. I tried ringing her yesterday for a chat, but I think she was away at her sister's.'

'I'll call round there this week,' Alice promised immediately. 'I was going to anyway.'

Betty smiled. 'Thank you, dear. You may not have been born here but you're a good girl and we're lucky to have you.' She turned to Gio with a girlish smile. 'And doubly lucky now, it seems.'

The couple left the surgery and Alice shook her head in disbelief. 'Well, you really charmed her. Congratulations. I've never seen Betty blush before. You've made a conquest.'

His gaze was swift and assessing. 'And that surprises you?'

'Well, let's put it this way—she's not known for her warmth to strangers unless they're spending money in her shop.'

'I thought she was a nice lady.' He switched off the light and tidied up the equipment he'd used. 'A bit cautious, but I suppose that's natural.'

'Welcome to Smuggler's Cove,' Alice said lightly. 'If you can't trace your family back for at least five generations, you're a stranger.'

'And how about you, Alice?' He paused and his dark gold eyes narrowed as they rested on her face. 'From her comments, you obviously aren't a local either. So far we've talked about work and nothing else. Tell me about yourself.'

His slow, seductive masculine tones slid over her taut nerves and soothed her. It was a voice designed to lull an unsuspecting woman into a sensual coma.

'Alice?'

Alice shook herself. She wasn't going to be thrown off her stride just because the man was movie-star handsome. She'd leave that to the rest of the female population of the village. 'There's nothing interesting to say about me. I'm very boring.'

'You mean you don't like talking about yourself.'

He was sharp, she had to give him that. 'I came here after I finished my GP rotation five years ago so, no, I don't qualify as a local,' she said crisply, delivering the facts as succinctly as possible. In her experience, the quickest way to stop someone asking questions was to answer a few. 'But I'm accepted because of the job I do.'

'And it's obviously a job you do very well. So where is home to you? Where are your family?'

Her blood went cold and all her muscles tightened. 'This is my home.'

There was a brief pause and when he spoke again his voice was gentle. 'Then you're lucky, because I can't think of a nicer place to live.' His eyes lingered on her face and then he strolled across the room to wash his hands. 'Do you often do night visits?'

Relieved that he'd changed the subject, some of the tension left her. 'Not since the new GP contract. Why?'

'Because I was told that the other night you were up with a child who had an asthma attack.'

'Chloe Bennett.' She frowned. 'How do you know that?'

He dried his hands. 'I was talking to the girl in the coffee-shop yesterday. Blonde. Nice smile.'

Alice resisted the temptation to roll her eyes. 'Katy Adams.' Obviously another conquest.

'Nice girl.'

Knowing Katy's reputation with men, Alice wondered if she should warn her new partner that he could be in mortal danger. She decided against it. A man who looked like him would have been fending off women from his cradle. He certainly wouldn't need any help from her.

'Chloe Bennett is a special case,' she explained briskly. 'Her mother has been working hard to control her asthma and give her some sort of normal life at school. It's been very difficult. She has my home number and I encourage her to use it when there's a problem, and that's what happened the night before last. I had to admit her in the end but not before she'd given me a few nasty moments.'

'I can't believe you give patients your home number.'

'Not every patient. But when the need is real…' She gave a shrug. 'It makes perfect sense from a management point of view. I'm the one with all the information. It means Chloe gets better care and her mother doesn't have to explain her history all the time.'

'You can't be there for everyone all the time. It isn't possible.'

'But continuity makes sense from a clinical point of view.' She frowned as she thought of it. 'In Chloe's case it means that a doctor unfamiliar with her case doesn't have to waste time taking details from a panicking parent when it's dark outside and the child can't breathe properly.'

'I can clearly see the benefits for your patients.' His eyes, dark and disturbingly intense, searched hers in a way that she found unsettling. 'But the benefits for you are less clear to me. It places an enormous demand on your time. On your life.'

'Yes, well, my job is important to me,' she said quickly, wondering whether there was anyone left in the world who felt the way she did about medicine. 'For me the job isn't about doing as little as possible and going home as early as possible. It's about involving yourself in the health of a community. About making a real difference to people's lives. I don't believe that a supermarket approach to health care is in anyone's interests.' She broke off and gave an awkward shrug, spots of colour touching her cheeks as she reflected on the fact that she was in danger of becoming carried away. 'Sorry. It's just something I feel strongly about. I don't expect you to understand. You probably think I'm totally mad.'

'On the contrary, I think your patients are very fortunate. But in all things there has to be compromise. How can you be awake to see patients—how can you be truly at your best—when you've been up half the night?' He strolled towards her and she felt her whole body tense in a response that she didn't understand.

She'd always considered herself to be taller than average but next to him she felt small. Even in heels she only reached his shoulder. Unable to help herself, she took a step backwards and then immediately wished she hadn't. 'You don't need to worry about me, Dr Moretti,' she said, keeping her tone cool and formal to compensate for her reaction. 'I'm not short of stamina and I really enjoy my life. And my patients certainly aren't suffering.'

'I'm sure they're not.' He gave a slow smile and raised an eyebrow. 'Does it make you feel safer, Alice?'

She took another step backwards. 'Does what make me feel safer?'

'Calling me Dr Moretti.' His expression was thoughtful. 'You do it whenever I get too close. Does it help give you the distance you need?'

She felt her heart pump harder. 'I don't know what you're talking about.'

'Was it a man?' He lifted a hand and tucked a strand of blonde hair behind her ear, his fingers lingering. 'Tell me, Alice. Was it a man who hurt you? Is that why you live alone and bury yourself in work? Is that why you don't believe in love?'

With a subtle movement that was entirely instinctive she moved her head away from his touch. 'You're obviously a romantic, Dr Moretti.'

'You're doing it again, *tesoro,*' he said softly, his hand

suspended in midair as he studied her face. 'Calling me Dr Moretti. It's Gio. And of course I'm romantic.'

'I'm sure you are.' She tilted her head, her smile mocking. 'All men are when it suits their purpose.'

He raised an eyebrow. 'You're suggesting that I use romance as some sort of seduction tool? You're a cynic, Alice, do you know that?'

Was it even worth defending herself? 'I'm a realist.' Her tone was cool. 'And you're clearly an extremely intelligent man. You should know better than to believe in all that woolly, emotional rubbish.'

'Ah, but you've overlooked one important fact about me.' His eyes gleamed dark and dangerous as he slid a hand under her chin and forced her to look at him. 'I'm Sicilian. We're a romantic race. It's in the blood. It has nothing to do with seduction and everything to do with a way of life. And a life is nothing without love in it.'

'Oh, please.' She rolled her eyes. 'I'm a scientist. I prefer to deal with the tangible. I happen to believe that love is a myth and the current divorce statistics would appear to support my view.'

'You think everything in this world can be explained given sufficient time in a laboratory?'

'Yes.' Her tone was cool and she brushed his hand away in a determined gesture. 'If it can't then it probably doesn't exist.'

'Is that right?' He looked at her as if he wanted to say something more but instead he smiled. 'So what do you do to relax around here? Restaurants? Watersports?'

For some reason her heart had set up a rhythmic pounding in her chest. 'I read a lot.'

'That sounds lonely, Dr Anderson,' he said softly. 'Especially for someone as young and beautiful as you.'

Taken aback and totally flustered, she raked a hand through her blonde hair and struggled for words. 'I—If you're flirting with me, Dr Moretti, it's only fair to warn you that you're wasting your time. I don't flirt. I don't play those sorts of games.'

'I wasn't flirting and I certainly wasn't playing games. I was stating a fact.' He said the words thoughtfully, his eyes narrowed as they scanned her face. 'You are beautiful. And very English. In Sicily, you would have to watch that pale skin.'

'Well, since I have no plans to visit Sicily, it isn't a problem that's likely to keep me awake at night.' Her head was buzzing and she felt completely on edge. There was something about him—something about the way he looked at her…

Deciding that the only way to end the conversation was to leave the room, she headed for the door.

'Wait. Don't run,' he said gently, his fingers covering hers before she could open the door.

His hand was hard. Strong. She turned, her heart pounding against her chest when she realised just how close he was.

'We have to meet Gina and—'

'What are you afraid of, Alice?'

'I'm not afraid. I'm just busy.' There was something in those dark eyes that brought a bubble of panic to her throat and her insides knotted with tension.

'You don't have to be guarded around me, Alice.' For a brief moment his fingers tightened on hers and then he let her go and took a step backwards, giving her the distance she craved. 'People interest me. There's often such a gulf between the person on the surface and the person underneath. It's rewarding to discover the real person.'

'Well, in my case there's nothing to discover, so don't waste your time.' She opened the door a crack. 'You're a good-looking guy, Dr Moretti, you don't need me to tell you that. I'm sure you can find no end of women willing to stroll on the beach with you, fall into bed, fall in love or do whatever it is you like to do in your spare time. You certainly don't need me. And now we need to meet Gina. She'll be waiting.'

CHAPTER SIX

GIO spent the rest of the day wondering about Alice. Wondering about her past.

She'd claimed that it hadn't been a man who'd forged her attitude to love, but it had to have been someone. In his experience, no one felt that strongly about relationships unless they'd been badly burned.

He tried to tell himself that it wasn't his business and that he wasn't interested. But he was interested. Very. And she filled his mind as he worked his way through a busy afternoon surgery.

The patients were a mix of locals and tourists and he handled them with ease and skill. Sore throats, arthritis, a diabetic who hadn't brought the right insulin on holiday and a nasty local reaction to an insect bite.

The locals lingered and asked questions. Where had he worked last? Had he bought a wife with him? Was he planning on staying long? The tourists were eager to leave the surgery and get on with their holiday.

Gio saw them all quickly and efficiently and handled the more intrusive questions as tactfully as possible, his mind distracted by thoughts of Alice. She was interesting, he mused as he checked glands and stared into throats. Interesting, beautiful and very serious.

Slightly prickly, wary, definitely putting up barriers. But underneath the front he sensed passion and vulnerability. He sensed that she was afraid.

He frowned slightly as he printed out a prescription for eye drops and handed it to his last patient.

There had been no mention of a social life in her description of relaxation. And David had definitely said that his partner had no time for anything other than work.

'You finished quickly today.' She walked into the room towards the end of the afternoon, just as his patient left. 'Any problems?'

'No. No problems so far.' He shook his head and leaned back in his chair. 'Should I have expected some?'

'People round here are congenitally nosy. You should have already realised that after twenty minutes in the company of the Normans this morning.' This time she stood near the door. Keeping a safe distance. 'This is a small, close-knit community and a new doctor is bound to attract a certain degree of attention. I bet they've been asking you no end of personal questions. Do you answer?'

'When it suits me. And when it doesn't…' he gave a shrug '…let's just say I was evasive. So, Dr Anderson, what next? I've asked about you but you haven't asked anything about me and you're probably the only one entitled to answers, given that we're working closely together.'

Their eyes met briefly and held for a long moment. Then she looked away. 'I've read your CV and that's all that matters. I'm not interested in the personal, Dr Moretti. Your life outside work is of no interest to me whatsoever. I really don't feel the need to know anything about you. You're doing your job. That's all I care about.'

Gio studied her in thoughtful silence. There was chemistry there. He'd felt it and he knew she'd felt it, too. Felt it and rejected it. Her face was shuttered. Closed. As if a protective shield had been drawn across her whole person.

Why?

'Make sure you have your key tonight because I have two house calls to make on the way home, so I'll be a bit late. Then I'm going to call at the supermarket and pick up the ingredients for a curry.' What exactly went into a curry? She knew she'd made it once before but she had no precise recollection of the recipe. 'How was the mother and baby clinic?'

'Fun. Interesting. But no Harriet.'

Alice frowned. 'Did you talk to Gina after our meeting?'

'At length. Interestingly enough, she's found it very hard to see Harriet. Every time she tries to arrange a visit Harriet makes an excuse, but she said that she'd sounded quite happy on the phone so she hasn't pushed. She thinks Harriet is just under a normal amount of strain for a new mother but she's promised to make another attempt at seeing her.'

'And what do you think?'

His gaze lifted to hers. 'After what I saw in the waiting room, I need to talk to her before I can answer that question.'

Alice grabbed her keys and popped her head into the nurse's room to say goodbye to Rita. 'I'm off. If Harriet comes to see you for anything in the next few days, make sure you encourage her to make an appointment with Dr Moretti.'

'I certainly will.' Rita returned a box of vaccines to the fridge and smiled. 'If you ask me, the man is a real find. Caring, warm and yet still incredibly masculine. You two have a nice evening together.'

'Don't you start. It isn't a date, Rita,' Alice said tightly. 'He's my lodger, thanks to Mary.'

Only somewhere along the way he'd forgotten his role. Lodgers weren't supposed to probe and delve and yet, from what she'd seen so far, Gio just couldn't help himself. Probing and delving seemed to be in his blood. Even with Harriet, he'd refused to take her insistence that she was fine at face value. Clearly he didn't intend to let the matter drop until he'd satisfied himself that she wasn't depressed.

Alice watched absently as Rita closed the fridge door. But, of course, at least where the patients were concerned, that was a good thing. It was his job to try and judge what was wrong with them. To pick up signs. Search for clues. To see past the obvious. She just didn't need him doing it with *her.*

'It's not Mary's fault the letting agency made a mess of things,' Rita said airily as she washed her hands. 'And if he were my lodger, I'd be thanking my lucky stars.'

'Well, you and I are different. And we both know that the letting agency wouldn't have made a mess of things without some significant help from certain people around here.' Alice put her hands on her hips and glared. 'And just for the record, in case you didn't get the message the first two hundred times, I don't need you to set me up with a man!'

'Don't you?' Rita dried her hands and dropped the paper towel in the bin. 'Strikes me you're not doing anything about it yourself.'

'Because, believe it or not, being with a man isn't compulsory!'

Reaching the point of explosion, Alice turned on her heel and strode out to her car before Rita had a chance to irritate her further. That day had been one long aggravation, she decided as she delved in her bag for her keys. All she wanted was to be left in peace to live her life the way she wanted to live it. What was so wrong with that?

Climbing into her car, she closed the door and shut her eyes.

Breathe, she told herself firmly, trying to calm herself down. Breathe. In and out. Relax.

Beside her, the door was pulled open. 'Alice, *tesoro,* are you all right?'

Her eyes opened. Gio was leaning into the car, his eyes concerned.

'I'm fine.' Gripping the wheel tightly, she wondered whether the sight of a GP screaming in a public place would attract attention. 'Or at least I will be fine when people stop interfering with my life and leave me alone. At least part of this is your fault.' She glared at him and his eyes narrowed.

'My fault?'

'Well, if you weren't single and good-looking, they wouldn't have been able to move you into my house.'

He rubbed a hand across his jaw and laughter flickered in his eyes. 'You want me to get married or rearrange my features?'

'No point. They'd just find some other poor individual to push my way.' Her tone gloomy, she slumped back in her seat and shook her head. 'Sorry, this really isn't your fault at all. It's just this place. Maybe David was right to get away. Right now I'd pay a lot to live among people who don't know who on earth I am and can't be bothered to find out. I must get going. I've got house calls to make on my way home.'

Unfortunately her car had other ideas. As she turned the key in the ignition the engine struggled and choked and then died.

'Oh, for crying out loud!' In a state of disbelief Alice glared at the car, as if fury alone should be enough to start it. 'What is happening to my life?'

Gio was still leaning on the open door. 'Do you often have problems with it?'

'Never before.' She tried the ignition again. 'My car is the only place I can get peace and quiet these days! The only place I can hide from people trying to pair me off with you! And now even that has died!'

'Shh.' He put a hand over her lips, his eyes amused. 'Calm down.'

'I can't calm down. I've got house calls to make and no transport.'

'I'm leaving now.' His tone was calm and reasonable as he gestured to the low, sleek sports car parked next to hers. 'We'll do the calls together.'

'But—'

'It makes perfect sense. It will help me orientate myself a little.'

'What's happening?' Mary hurried up, a worried expression on her face. 'Is it your car?'

'Yes.' Alice hissed the word through gritted teeth. 'It's my car.'

'Give me the keys and I'll get it taken care of,' Mary said immediately, holding out her hand. 'I'll call Paul at the garage. He's a genius with cars. In the meantime, you go with Dr Moretti.'

A nasty suspicion unfolded like a bud inside her. 'Mary…' Alice shook her head and decided she was becoming paranoid. No matter how much Mary wanted to push her towards Gio, she wasn't capable of tampering with a car. 'All right. Thanks.'

Accepting defeat, she climbed out of her car, handed the keys to Mary and slid into Gio's black sports car.

He pressed a button and the roof above her disappeared in a smooth movement.

She rolled her eyes. 'Show-off.'

He gave her a boyish grin, slid sunglasses over his eyes and reversed out of the parking space.

The last thing she saw as they pulled out of the surgery car park was the smug expression on Mary's face.

He drove up the hill, away from the harbour, with Alice giving directions.

'I'm embarrassed turning up at house calls in this car,' she mumbled as they reached the row of terraced houses where Edith lived. 'It's hardly subtle, is it? Everyone will think I've gone mad.'

'They will be envious and you will give them something interesting to talk about. Is this the lady that Betty was talking about earlier?' Gio brought the car to a halt and switched off the engine.

'Yes. Edith Carne.' Alice reached for her bag. 'She's

one of David's patients but she had a fall a few weeks ago and I just want to check on her because she lives on her own and she's not one to complain. You don't have to come with me. You're welcome to wait in the car. Who knows? Keep the glasses on and you might get lucky with some passing female.'

'But I am already lucky,' he said smoothly, leaning across to open the door for her, 'because you are in my car, *tesoro.*'

She caught the wicked twinkle in his dark eyes and pulled a face. 'Save the charm, Romeo. It's wasted on me.' She climbed out of the car and walked towards the house, her hair swinging around her shoulders, frustration still bubbling inside her.

'If she's David's patient, she's going to be mine,' Gio pointed out as he caught up with her, 'so this is as good a time as any to make her acquaintance. It's logical.'

It was logical, but still she would have rather he'd waited in the car. Having him tailing her flustered her and put her on edge. She needed space to calm herself. Normally she loved her work and found it absorbing and relaxing but today she felt restless and unsettled, as if the door to her tidy, ordered life had been flung wide open.

And it was all thanks to Mary and Rita, she thought angrily, and their interfering ways.

If she hadn't been living with the man, she could have easily avoided him. The surgery was so busy that often their paths didn't often cross during the day.

The evenings were a different matter.

Pushing aside feelings that she didn't understand, she rang the doorbell and waited. 'Her husband died three years ago,' she told Gio, 'and they were married for fifty-two years.'

He raised an eyebrow. 'And you don't believe in love?'

'There are lots of reasons why two people stay together.' She tilted her head back and stared up at the bedroom window through narrowed eyes. 'But love doesn't come into it, in my opinion. Why isn't she answering?'

'Does she have family?'

'No. But she has lots of friends in the village. She's lived here all her life.' Alice rang the bell again, an uneasy feeling spreading through her.

'Why did she fall last time? Does anyone know?'

'I don't think they found anything. The neighbour called an ambulance. She had a few cuts and bruises but nothing broken. But I know David was worried about her.' And now she was worried, too. Why wasn't Edith answering the door? She sighed and jammed her fingers through her hair. 'All right. I suppose I'll have to go next door and get the key, but I hate the thought of doing that.' Hated the thought of invading another person's privacy.

'Could she have gone out?' Gio stepped across the front lawn and glanced in through the front window. 'I can hear voices. A television maybe? But I can't see anyone.'

Alice was on the point of going next door to speak to the neighbour when the door opened.

'Oh, Edith.' She gave a smile of relief as she saw the old lady standing there. 'We were worried about you. We thought you might have fallen again. I wanted to check on how you're feeling.'

'Well, that's kind of you but I'm fine, dear.' Edith was wearing a dressing-gown even though it was late afternoon, and the expression on her face was bemused. 'No problems at all.'

Alice scanned Edith's face, noting that she looked extremely pale and tired. Something wasn't right.

'Can I come in for a minute, Edith? I'd really like to have a chat and check that everything's all right with you. And I need to introduce you to our new doctor.' She flapped a hand towards Gio. 'He's taken over from David. Come all the way from Sicily. Land of *canolli* and volcanoes that misbehave.'

'Sicily? Frank and I went there once. It was beautiful.' Edith's knuckles whitened on the edge of the door. 'I'm fine, Dr Anderson. I don't need to waste your time. There's plenty worse off than me.'

'Consider it a favour to me.' Gio's voice was deep and heavily accented. 'I am new to the area, Mrs Carne. I need inside information and I understand you've lived here all your life.'

'Well, I have, but—'

'Please—I would be so grateful.' He spread his hands, his warm smile irresistible to any female, and Edith looked into his dark eyes and capitulated.

'All right, but I'm fine. Completely fine.'

At least Gio used his charm on the old as well as the young, Alice thought as they followed Edith into the house. Wondering whether she was the only one who felt that something wasn't right, she glanced at Gio but his attention was focused on the old lady.

'This is a lovely room.' His eyes scanned the ancient, rose-coloured sofa and the photographs placed three deep on the window-sill. 'I can see that it is filled with happy memories.'

'I was born in this house.' Edith sat down, folded her hands in her lap and stared at the empty fireplace. 'My parents died in this house and Frank and I carried on living here. I've lived here all my life. I can see the sea from my kitchen window.'

'It's a beautiful position.' Gio leaned towards a photograph displayed on a table next to his right hand. 'This is you? Was it taken in the garden of this house?'

Edith gave a nod and a soft smile. 'With my parents. I was five years old.' She stared wistfully at the photo, her hands clasped in her lap. 'The garden was different then, of course. My Frank loved the garden. I used to joke that he loved his plants more than me.'

Gio lifted the photo and took a closer look. 'It must be lovely to walk in the garden that he planted.'

Alice shifted impatiently in her chair. What was he talking about? And why wasn't he asking Edith questions about her blood pressure and whether she'd felt dizzy lately? What was the relevance of the garden, for goodness' sake?

Edith was staring at him, a strange expression in her eyes. 'Very few people understand how personal a garden can be.'

'A garden tells you so much about a person,' Gio agreed, replacing the photo carefully on the table. 'And being there, you share in their vision.'

Edith twisted her hands in her lap. 'Just walking there makes me feel close to him.'

Alice frowned, wondering where the conversation was leading. True, Edith was much more relaxed than she'd been when they'd arrived and she had to admit that Gio had a way with people, but why were they talking about gardening? She wanted to establish some facts. She wanted to find out whether Edith had suffered another fall but Gio seemed to be going down an entirely different path.

She forced herself to sit quietly and breathed an inaudible sigh of relief when Gio eventually steered the talk round to the topic of Edith's health. It was so skillfully done that it seemed like a natural direction for the conversation.

'I can barely remember the fall now,' Edith said dismissively, 'it was so long ago.'

'A month, Edith,' Alice reminded her, and the old lady sniffed, all the tension suddenly returning to her slim frame.

'I was just clumsy. Not looking where I was going. Tripped over the carpet. It won't happen again—I'm being really careful.'

Alice glanced around the room. The carpet was fitted. There were no rugs. The carpet in the hall and on the stairs had been fitted, too. Her eyes clashed with Gio's and she knew that he'd noticed the same thing.

'Can I just check your pulse and blood pressure?' He opened his bag and removed the necessary equipment. 'Just routine.'

'I suppose so…'

Gio pushed up the sleeve of her dressing-gown and paused. 'That's a nasty bruise on your arm,' he commented as he wrapped the blood-pressure cuff around her arm. 'Did you knock yourself?'

Edith didn't look at him. 'Just being a bit careless walking through the doorway.'

Without further comment Gio checked her pulse, blood

pressure and pulse and then eased the stethoscope out of his ears. 'When you went into hospital after your fall, did anyone say that your blood pressure was on the low side?'

Edith shook her head. 'Not that I remember. They just sent me home and told me they'd set up another appointment in a few months. I'm fine. Really I am. But it was good of you to call in.' She stood up, the movement quite agitated. 'I'll come to the surgery if I need any help. Good of you to introduce yourself.'

Not giving them a chance to linger, she hurried them out of the front door and closed it.

'Well.' Standing on the doorstep, staring at a closed door, Alice blinked in amazement. 'What was all that about? She's normally the most hospitable woman in the community. From her reaction today, you would have thought we were planning to take her away and lock her up.'

'I think that's exactly what she thought.' Gio turned and walked down the path towards his car.

'What do you mean?' She caught up with him in a few strides. 'You're not making sense.'

He unlocked the car doors. 'I think your Mrs Carne has had more falls since David saw her. But she isn't ready to confess.' He slid into the car while Alice gaped at him from the pavement.

'But why?' It seemed simple to Alice. 'If she's falling then she should tell us and we'll try and solve it.'

The engine gave a throaty roar and he drummed long fingers on the steering-wheel while he waited for her to get into the passenger seat. 'Life isn't always that simple, is it?'

She climbed in next to him and fastened her seat belt. 'So why wouldn't she tell us?'

'General practice is very like detective work, don't you think?' He glanced towards her. 'In hospital you see only the patient. At home you have the advantage of seeing the patient in their own environment and that often contains clues about the person they are. About the way they live their lives.'

'And what clues did you see?'

'That her whole life is contained in that house. There were photographs of her parents, her as a child, her husband. There were cushions that she'd knitted on a sofa that I'm willing to bet belonged to her mother. The garden had been planted by her husband.'

Alice tried to grasp the relevance of what he was saying and failed. 'But that's all emotional stuff. What's that got to do with her illness?'

'Not everything about a patient can be explained by science alone, Alice.' He checked the rear-view mirror and pulled out. 'She doesn't want us to know she's falling because she's afraid we're going to insist she leaves her home. And she loves her home. Her home is everything to her. It contains all her memories. Take her from it and you erase part of her life. Probably the only part that matters.'

He was doing it again, Alice mused, delving deep. Refusing to accept people at face value.

She stared ahead as he drove off down the quiet road and back onto the main road. 'Take a left here,' she said absently, her mind still on their conversation. 'Aren't you making it complicated? I mean, if Edith is falling, we need to find the reason. It's that simple. The rest isn't really anything to do with us.'

'The rest is everything to do with us if it affects the patient. You're very afraid of emotions, aren't you, Alice?' His voice was soft and she gave a frown.

'We're not talking about me.'

'Of course we're not.' There was no missing the irony in his tone but she chose to ignore it.

'So now what do we do?'

'I want to check on a couple of things. Look at the correspondence that came out of her last appointment and speak to the doctor who saw her before I go crashing in with my diagnosis.'

'Which is?' The wind picked up a strand of hair and blew it across her face. 'You think you know why she's falling?'

'Not for sure, no. But certainly there are clues.' He eased the car round a tight corner, his strong hands firm on the wheel. 'Her heart rate is on the slow side and her blood pressure is low. What do you know about CSS?'

'Carotid sinus syndrome. I remember reading a UK study on it a few years ago.' Alice sifted through her memory and her brow cleared. 'They linked it to unexplained falls in the elderly. It can result in syncope—fainting. Are you saying that you think—?' She broke off and Gio gave a shrug that betrayed his Latin heritage.

'I don't know for sure, of course, but it's certainly worth considering. It's important that elderly patients who fall are given cardiovascular assessment. Do you think this happened in her case?'

'Not to my knowledge. We'll check the notes and, if not, we'll refer her immediately.' The wind teased her hair again and Alice slid a hand through the silky strands and tried to anchor them down. 'Well done. That was very smart of you. And all that stuff about her house and the way she was feeling…' She frowned, angry and disappointed with herself. 'I wouldn't have thought of that.'

'That's because you work only with facts and not emotions, but the truth is that the two work together. You can't dissociate them from each other, Alice. Emotions are a part of people's lives.' He gave her a quick glance, a slight smile touching his mouth, a challenge in his dark eyes. 'And she was definitely in love with her husband.'

She tipped her head back against the seat and rolled her eyes upwards. 'Don't let's go there again.'

'You heard the way she talked about him. You saw the look on her face. Do you really think she didn't love him?'

'Well, obviously you're going to miss someone if you've lived with them for over fifty years,' Alice said tetchily, 'and I'm sure they were best friends. I just don't believe in this special, indefinable, woolly emotion that supposedly binds two people together.'

'You don't believe in love at first sight?'

'Nor on second or third sight,' Alice said dryly, letting go of her hair and pointing a finger towards a turning. 'You need to take a right down there so that I can pick up some dinner.'

He followed her instructions and turned into the supermarket car park. 'Listen, about dinner. You cooked last night. Perhaps I ought to—'

'No need. I've got it. Back in five minutes.' She slammed the door and braced herself for her second least favourite pastime after cooking. Shopping for the ingredients.

* * *

Later, wondering whether his taste buds would ever recover, Gio drank yet another glass of water in an attempt to quench the fire burning in his mouth. 'Alice, tomorrow it's my turn to cook.'

'Why would you want to do that?'

Was it all right to be honest? He gave a wry smile and risked it. 'Because I want to live?'

Because he respected his stomach far too much to eat another one of her meals and because he needed to show her that there was more to eating than simply ingesting animal and plant material in any format.

She sighed and dropped her fork. 'All right, it tasted pretty awful but I'm not that great at curry. I think I might have got my tablespoons mixed up with my tea-spoons. Does it really matter?'

'When you're measuring chilli powder? Yes,' he replied dryly. 'And, anyway, I'm very happy to cook from now on. I love to cook. I'll do you something Italian. You'll enjoy it.'

She pushed her plate away, the contents only half-eaten. 'We eat to live, Gio, not the other way round. The body needs protein, carbohydrate, fats and all that jazz in order to function the way it should. It doesn't care how you throw them together.'

She was all fact, he thought to himself. All fact and science. As far as she was concerned, if it couldn't be explained by some fancy theory then it didn't exist.

It would be fun to show her just what could be achieved with food, he decided. And atmosphere.

At least she'd stopped jumping every time he walked into the room. It was time to make some changes. Time to push her out of her comfort zone.

He tapped his foot under the table, his mind working. Maybe it was time to show Dr Alice Anderson that there was more to life than scientific theory. That not everything could be proven.

Maybe it was time for her to question her firmly held beliefs. But before that he needed to deal with his indigestion.

'Let's go for a walk on the beach.'

She shook her head and dumped the remains of the totally inedible curry in the bin. 'I need to catch up on some reading. You go. Take a left at the bottom of the garden, along the cycle path for about two hundred metres and you reach the harbour. Go to the end and you drop straight down onto the beach. You can walk for miles if the tide is out. Once it comes in you have to scramble up the cliffs to the coast path.'

'I want you to come with me.' Not giving her a chance to shrink away from him, he reached out a hand and dragged her to her feet. 'The reading can wait.'

'I really need to…' Her hand wriggled in his as she tried to pull away, but he kept a tight hold and used his trump card. Work.

'I want to talk about some of David's patients.' He kept his expression serious. Tried to look suitably concerned. 'It's obvious to me that the only time we're going to have for discussion is during the evenings. And I have so many questions.'

He struggled to think of a few, just in case he needed to produce one.

'Oh.' She thought for a moment and then gave a shrug. 'Well, I suppose that makes sense, but we don't have to go out. We could do it here and—'

'Alice, we've been trapped inside all day. We both need some air.' Letting go of her hand, he reached out and grabbed her jacket from the back of the door. 'Let's walk.'

'Have you come across a specific problem with a patient? Who is on your mind?'

He racked his brains to find someone to talk about, knowing that if he didn't start talking about work immediately, she'd vanish upstairs and spend the rest of the evening with her journals and textbooks, as she had the previous evening.

'I thought we could talk about the right way to approach Harriet.' He stepped through the back door and waited while she locked it. 'You know her after all.'

'Not that well. She was David's patient. Mary knows her, she might have some ideas.'

She slipped the keys into her pocket and they walked down to the cycle way. Although it was still only early evening, several cyclists sped past them, enjoying the summer weather and the wonderful views.

The tide was far out, leaving sandbanks exposed in the water.

'It's beautiful.' Gio stared at the islands of sand and Alice followed his gaze.

'Yes. And dangerous. The tide comes in so fast, it's lethal.' She stepped to one side to avoid another cyclist. 'There are warnings all over the harbour and the beach, but still some tourists insist on dicing with death. Still, it keeps the lifeboat busy.'

They reached the harbour and weaved a path through the crowds of tourists who were milling around, watch-

ing the boats and eating fish and chips on the edge of
the quay.

Gio slipped a hand in his pocket. 'Ice cream, Dr
Anderson?'

'I don't eat ice cream.' She was looking around her
with a frown. 'Bother. We shouldn't have come this way.'

'Why not?'

'Because I've just seen at least half a dozen people
who know me.'

'And what's wrong with that?' He strolled over to the
nearest ice-cream shop and scanned the menu. Vanilla?
Too boring. Strawberry? Too predictable.

'Because if I've seen them, then they've seen me.'
She turned her head. 'With you.'

'Ah.' Cappuccino, he decided. 'And surely that's a
good thing.'

'Why would fuelling town gossip possibly be a
good thing?'

'Because you want to prove that you don't want a relationship.' He wandered into the shop and ordered two
cones. 'In order to do that, you at least have to be seen
to be mixing with members of the opposite sex. If you
do that and still don't fall in love then eventually everyone will just give up trying. If you don't, they'll just
keep fixing you up.'

She glared at him and he realised that the lady selling
the ice creams was listening avidly.

'Perfect evening for a walk, Dr Anderson. We don't
see you in here often enough. That will be three pounds
forty, please.' The woman took the money with a smile
and turned to Gio. 'You must be our new doctor. Betty
told me all about you.'

'That's good. Saves me introducing myself.' Gio pocketed the change and picked up the ice creams with a nod of thanks and a few more words of small talk.

Outside he handed a cone to Alice.

'I said I didn't want one.'

'Just try it. One lick.'

'It's—'

'It's protein, Dr Anderson.' He winked at her and she raised an eyebrow.

'How do you work that out?'

'All that clotted cream.' He watched, noting with satisfaction the smile that teased the corners of her mouth. He was going to teach her to relax. To loosen up. To enjoy herself.

'It's a frozen lump of saturated fat designed to occlude arteries,' she said crisply, and he nodded.

'Very possibly. But it's also a mood lifter. An indulgence. A sensory experience. Smooth. Cold. Creamy. Try it.'

She stared at him. 'It's ice cream, Gio. Just ice cream.' She waved a hand dismissively and almost consigned the ice cream to the gutter. 'The body doesn't need ice cream in order to function efficiently.'

'The body may not *need* ice cream,' he conceded, 'but it's extremely grateful to receive it. Try it and find out. Go on—lick.'

With an exaggerated roll of her eyes she licked the cone. And licked again. 'All right, so it tastes good. But that's just because of the coffee. You know I love coffee.' The evening sunlight caught the gold in her hair and her blue eyes were alight with humour. 'It's my only vice.'

Looking at the way her mouth moved over the ice cream, he decided that before the summer was finished Alice would have expanded her repertoire of vices. And he was going to help her do it.

'Lick again and close your eyes,' he urged her, ignoring the fact that his own ice cream was in grave danger of melting.

She stared at him as if he were mad. 'Gio, I'm not closing my eyes with half the town watching! I have to work with these people long after you've gone! I need to retain my credibility. If I stand in the harbour with my eyes closed, licking ice cream, they'll never listen to me again.'

'Stop trying to be so perfect all the time. And stop worrying about other people.' She was delightfully prim, he thought, noticing the tiny freckles on her nose for the first time. He doubted she'd ever let her hair down in her life.

And he was absolutely crazy about her.

The knowledge knocked the breath from his lungs. 'Close your eyes, or I'll throw you in the harbour.' His voice was gruff. 'And that will seriously damage your credibility.'

How could he possibly be in love with a woman he'd only known for a couple of days?

'Oh, fine!' With an exaggerated movement she squeezed her eyes shut and he stepped closer, tempted by the slight pout of her lips.

Suppressing the desire to kiss her until her body melted like the ice cream in her hand, he reminded himself that it was too soon for her.

He was going to take it slowly. Take his time. *Coax her out of her shell.*

'Now lick again and tell me what you taste. Tell me what it makes you feel. What it reminds you of.'

Her lick was most definitely reluctant. 'Ice cream?' Receiving no response to her sarcasm, she licked again and he waited. And waited. But she said nothing.

'Don't you go straight back to your childhood?' He decided that he was going to have to prompt her. Clearly she'd never played this game before. 'Seaside holidays, relaxation? All the fun of being young?'

There was a long silence and then her eyes opened and for a brief moment he saw the real Alice. And what he saw shocked and silenced him. He saw pain and anguish. He saw hurt and disillusionment. But most of all he saw a child who was lost and vulnerable. Alone.

And then she blanked it.

'No, Dr Moretti.' Her voice had a strange, rasping quality, as if talking was suddenly difficult. 'I don't see that. And I'm not that keen on ice cream.' Without giving him time to reply, she tossed it in the nearest bin and made for the beach, virtually breaking into a run in her attempt to put distance between them.

CHAPTER SEVEN

AT THE bottom of the path, Alice slowed her pace and took several gulps of air. Her stomach churned and she felt light-headed and sick but most of all she felt angry with herself for losing control.

Oh, damn, damn damn.

How could she have let that happen? How could she have revealed so much? And because she had, *because she'd been so stupid,* he was going to come after her and demand an explanation. He was that sort of man. The sort of man who always looked beneath the surface. The sort of man who delved and dug until he had access to all parts of a person.

And she didn't want him delving. She didn't want him digging.

She bent down, removed her shoes and stepped onto the sand, intending to walk as far as possible, as fast as possible. *Even though she knew that even if she were to run, it wouldn't make any difference.* The problems were inside her and always would be, and she knew from experience that running couldn't change the past. Couldn't change the feelings that were part of her.

But she'd learned ways to handle them, she reminded

herself firmly as she breathed in deeply and unclenched her hands. Ways that worked for her. It was just a question of getting control back. Of being the person she'd become.

She stared at the sea, watching the yachts streak across the bay, the wind filling their brightly coloured sails. Breathing in the same strong sea breeze, she struggled to find the familiar feeling of calm, but it eluded her.

She was concentrating so hard on breathing that the feel of Gio's hand on her shoulder made her jump, even though she'd been expecting it.

Her instinct was to push him away, but that would draw attention that she didn't want. She could have run but that, she told herself, would just make it even harder later. It would just delay the inevitable conversation. So she decided to stay put and give him enough facts to satisfy him. Just enough and no more.

She turned to face him and dislodged his hand in the process. Immediately she wished she'd thought to wear sunglasses. Or a wide-brimmed hat. Anything to give her some protection from that searching, masculine gaze.

She felt exposed. Naked.

Wishing she'd decided to run, she hugged herself with her arms and looked away, gesturing towards the beach with a quick jerk of her head. 'You can walk along here for about an hour before the tide turns.' The words spilled out like girlish chatter. 'Then you have to climb up to the coast path if you don't want to get cut off.'

'Alice—'

'It's a nice walk and you always lose the crowds about ten minutes out of the harbour.' The wind picked up a strand of her hair and threw it across her face, but she ignored it. 'It will take you about an hour and a half to reach the headland.'

He stepped closer and his hands closed over her arms. 'Alice, don't!' He gave her a little shake. 'Don't shut me out like this. I said something to upset you and for that I'm sorry.'

'You don't need to be sorry. You haven't done anything wrong.' She tilted her head back and risked another glance at his face. And saw kindness. Kindness and sympathy. The combination untwisted something that had been knotted inside her for years and she very nearly let everything spill out. Very nearly told him exactly how she was feeling. But she stopped herself. Reminded herself of how she'd chosen to live her life. 'I just don't happen to like ice cream that much.'

'Alice…' He tried to hold her but she shrugged him off, swamped by feelings that she didn't want to feel.

'I'm sorry, but I need to walk.'

He muttered something in Italian and then switched to English. 'Alice, wait!' With his long stride, he caught up with her easily. 'We need to talk.' His Italian accent was stronger than ever, as if he was struggling with the language.

'We don't need to talk.' She walked briskly along the sand, her shoes in one hand, the other holding her hair out of her eyes. This far up the beach the sand was soft and warm, cushioning the steady rhythm of her feet and causing her to stumble occasionally. 'I don't want to talk! Not everyone wants to talk about everything, Gio.'

'Because you're afraid of your own emotions. Of being hurt. That's why you prefer facts.' He strode next to her, keeping pace. 'You've turned yourself into a machine, Alice, but emotions are the oil that makes the machine work. Human beings can't function without emotions.'

She walked faster in an attempt to escape the conversation. 'You don't need to get into my skin and understand me. And I don't need healing.'

'Most people need healing from something, Alice. It's—*Dios,* can you stop walking for a moment?' Reaching out, he grabbed her shoulders and turned her, his fingers firm on her flesh as he held her still. 'Stop running and have a conversation. Is that really so frightening?'

'You want facts? All right, I'll give you the facts. You and Edith obviously have lots of happy childhood memories. I don't.' Her heart thumped steadily against her chest as her past spilled into her present. 'It's as simple as that. Ice cream doesn't remind me of happy holidays, Gio. It reminds me of bribes. A way of persuading me to like my mother's latest boyfriend. A way of occupying me for ten minutes while my father spent romantic time with his latest girlfriend. Ice cream was a salve to the conscience while they told me I needed to live in a different place for a while because I was getting in the way of *"love"*.' Her heart was beating, her palms were sweaty and feelings of panic bubbled up inside her. Feelings that she hadn't had for a very long time.

Gio sucked in a breath. 'This was your childhood?'

'Sometimes I was a ping-pong ball, occasionally I was a pawn but mostly I was just a nuisance.'

'And now?' He frowned and his grip on her arms tightened. 'Your parents are divorced?'

'Oh, several times. Not just the once.' She knew her tone was sarcastic and brittle but she couldn't do anything about it. Couldn't be bothered to hide it any more. Maybe if he understood the reasons for the way she was, he'd leave her alone. 'You know what they say—practice makes perfect. My parents had plenty of practice. They are quite expert at divorce.'

His eyes were steady on her face. Searching. 'And you?'

'Me? I survived.' She spread her hands. 'Here I am. In one piece.'

He shook his head. 'Not in one piece. Your belief in love has been shattered. They took that from you with their selfish behaviour.' He lifted a hand and touched her cheek. 'My beautiful Alice.'

Her breathing hitched in her throat and her shoulders stiffened. 'Don't feel sorry for me. I like my life. I don't need fairy-tales to be happy.' She tensed still further as he slid a hand over her cheek, his thumb stroking gently. 'What are you doing?'

'Offering you comfort. A hug goes a long way to making things better, don't you think?' His voice was soft. 'Touch is important.'

'I'm not used to being touched.' She stood rigid, not moving a muscle. 'I don't like being touched.'

'Then you need more practice. Everyone likes being touched, as long as it's in the right way.'

He was too close and it made her feel strange. His voice made her feel strange.

'Enough.' Shaken and flustered, she took a step backwards. Broke the contact. 'You just can't help it, can you? I've only known you for a short time but during that time I've seen how you always have to dig and delve into a person's life.'

'Because the answers to questions often lie below the surface.'

She scraped her hair out of her eyes. 'Well, I don't need you to delve and I don't want you to dig. There are no questions about my life that you need to answer. I'm not one of your patients with emotional needs.'

'Everyone has emotional needs, Alice.'

'Well, I don't. And I don't have to explain myself to you! And I don't need you to understand me. I didn't ask to take this walk and I didn't ask for your company. If you don't like the way I am then you can go back to the house.'

'I like the way you are, *cara mia*.' Without warning or hesitation, his hands cupped her face and he brought his mouth down on hers, his kiss warm and purposeful.

Alice stood there, frozen with shock while his mouth moved over hers, coaxing, tempting, growing more demanding, and suddenly a tiny, icy part of herself started to melt. The warmth started to spread and grew in intensity until she felt something explode inside her. Something delicious and exciting that she'd never felt before.

Feeling oddly disconnected, she tried to summon up logic and reason. *Any minute now she was going to pull away.* But his arms slid round her, his hold strong and powerful, and still his mouth plundered and stole the breath from her body. *She was going to punch him somewhere painful.* But his fingers stroked her cheek and his tongue teased and danced and coaxed a response that she'd never given to any man before.

In the end it was Gio who suspended the kiss. 'My Alice.' He lifted his head just enough to breathe the words against her mouth. 'They hurt you badly, *tesoro*.'

She felt dazed. Drugged. Unable to speak or think. She tried to open her eyes but her eyelids felt heavy, and as for her knees—hadn't David said something about knees?

'Dr Anderson!' A sharp young voice from directly behind her succeeded where logic had not. Her eyes opened and she pulled away, heart thumping, cheeks flaming.

'Henry?' Her voice cracked as she turned to acknowledge the ten-year-old boy behind her. Flustered and embarrassed, she stroked a hand over her cheeks in an attempt to calm herself down. 'What's the matter?'

Henry pointed, his expression frantic. 'They're cut off, Dr Anderson. The tide's turning.'

Beside her, Gio ran a hand over the back of his neck and she had the satisfaction of seeing that he was no more composed than she was.

For a brief, intense moment their eyes held and then she turned her attention back to Henry, trying desperately to concentrate on what he was saying.

And it was obviously something important. He was hopping on the spot, his expression frantic, his arms waving wildly towards the sea.

'Who is cut off from what?' She winced inwardly as she listened to herself. Since when had she been unable to form words properly? To focus on a problem in hand?

'The twins. They were playing.'

'Twins?' Alice shielded her eyes from the evening sun and stared out across the beach, her eyes drawn to two tiny figures playing on a small, raised patch of sand. All around them the sea licked and swirled, closing off their route back to the beach. They were on a sand spit and the tide was turning. 'Oh, no…'

Finally she understood what Henry had been trying to tell her and she slid her hand in her pocket and reached for her mobile phone even as she started to run towards the water. 'I'll call the coastguard. Where's their mother, Henry? Have you seen Harriet?' She was dialling as she spoke, her finger shaking as she punched in the numbers, aware that Gio was beside her, stripping off as he ran.

The boy shook his head, breathless. 'They were on their own, I think.'

Alice spoke to the coastguard, her communication brief and succinct, and then broke the connection and glanced around her. They couldn't possibly have been on their own. They were five years old. Harriet was a good mother. She wouldn't have left them.

And then she saw her, carrying the baby and weighed down by paraphernalia, walking along the beach and calling for the twins. Searching. She hadn't seen them. Hadn't seen the danger. And Alice could hear the frantic worry in her voice as she called.

'You go to Harriet, I'll get the twins,' Gio ordered, running towards the sea, his long, muscular legs closing the distance.

The tide was still far out but she knew how fast it came in, how quickly those tempting little sand spits disappeared under volumes of seawater.

She ran with him, aware that Henry was keeping up with them. 'Henry, go to the cliff and get us a line.' She barked out the instruction, her throat dry with fear, her heart pounding. 'You know the line with the lifebuoy.' She knew the dangers of entering the water without a buoyancy aid. 'Gio, wait. You have to wait. You can't just go in there.'

For a moment the kiss was forgotten. The ice cream was forgotten. Nothing mattered except the urgency of the moment. Two little boys in mortal danger. *The weight of responsibility.*

'In a few more minutes those children will be out of reach.'

Alice grabbed his arm as they ran. Tried to slow him. Tried to talk sense into him. The sand was rock hard now as they approached the water's edge and then finally she felt the damp lick of the sea against her toes and stopped. 'You're not going into that water without a line. Do you know how many people drown in these waters, trying to save others?' Her eyes skimmed his body, noticed the hard, well-formed muscles. He had the body of an athlete and at the moment it was clad only in a pair of black boxer shorts.

'Stop giving me facts, Alice.' His expression was grim. 'They're five years old,' he said roughly, 'and they're not going to stand like sensible children on that spit of sand and wait to be rescued. What do you want me to do? Watch while they drown? Watch while they die?' Concern thickened his accent and she shook her head.

'No, but—'

'Get me a buoyancy aid and go to Harriet,' he urged as he stepped into the water. He caught her arm briefly, his eyes on her face. 'And remember emotions when you talk to her, Alice. It isn't always about facts.'

He released her and Alice swallowed and cast a frantic glance up the coast. She knew the lifeboat would come from that direction. Or maybe the coastguard would send the helicopter. Either way, she knew they needed to hurry.

From the moment he plunged into the water she could see that Gio was a strong swimmer, but she knew that the tides in this part of the bay were lethal and she knew that it would only take minutes for the water level to rise. Soon the spit of sand that was providing the twins with sanctuary would vanish from under their feet.

She could hear them screaming and crying and closed her eyes briefly. And then she heard Harriet's cry of horror.

'Oh, my God—my babies.' The young mother covered her mouth with her hand, her breathing so rapid that Alice was afraid she might faint.

'Harriet—try and stay calm.' *What a stupid, useless thing to say to a mother whose two children were in danger of drowning.* She took refuge in facts, as she always did. 'We've called the coastguard and Dr Moretti is going to swim out to them. Henry Fox is getting the buoyancy aid.'

'Neither of them can swim,' Harriet gasped, her eyes wild with panic, and Alice remembered what Gio had said about remembering emotions.

She swallowed and felt helpless. She just wasn't in tune with other people's emotions. She wasn't comfortable. What would Gio say? Certainly not that the ability to swim wouldn't save the twins in the lethal waters of Smuggler's Cove.

'They don't need to swim because the coastguard is going to be here in a moment,' she said finally, jabbing her fingers into her hair and wishing she was better with words. She just didn't know the right things to say. And then she remembered what Gio had said about touch. Hesitantly she stepped closer to Harriet and slipped an arm round her shoulders.

Instantly Harriet turned towards her and clung. 'Oh, Dr Anderson, this is all my fault. I'm a useless mother. Terrible.'

Caught in the full flood of Harriet's emotion, Alice froze and wished for a moment that she'd been the one to go in the water. She would have been much better at dealing with tides than with an emotional torrent.

'You're a brilliant mother, Harriet,' she said firmly. 'The twins are beautifully mannered, tidy, the baby is fed—'

'But that isn't really what being a mother is,' Harriet sniffed, still clinging to Alice. 'A childminder can do any of those things. Being a mother is noticing what your child really needs. It's the fun stuff. The interaction. And I'm so tired, I just can't do any of it. They wanted to go to the beach so I took them, but I was too tired to actually play with them so I sat feeding the baby and then I just lost sight of them and they wandered off.'

Alice watched as Gio climbed onto another sand spit. Between him and the twins was one more strip of water. Treacherous water.

And then she heard the clack, clack, clack of an approaching helicopter and breathed a sigh of relief. Gio didn't even need to cross the water now. The coastguard could—

'No! Oh, no, don't try and get in the water,' Harriet shrieked, moving away from Alice and running towards the water's edge. 'Oh, Dr Anderson, my Dan is trying to get into the water.'

Gio saw it too and shouted something to the boys before diving into the sea to cross the last strip of water. He used a powerful front crawl but even so Alice could see that he was being dragged sideways by the fast current.

It was only after he pulled himself safely onto the strip of sand that Alice realised that her fingernails had cut into her palms.

She saw him lift one of the twins and take the other by the hand, holding them firmly while the coastguard helicopter hovered in position above them.

The sand was gradually disappearing as the tide swirled and reclaimed the land, and a crowd of onlookers had gathered on the beach and were watching the drama unfold.

Alice bit her lip hard. The helicopter crew would rescue them all. Of course they would.

Still with her arm round Harriet, she watched as the winchman was lowered down to the sand to collect the first child.

The baby was screaming in Harriet's arms but she just jiggled it vaguely, all her attention focused on her twins.

'Let me take her.' Alice reached across and took the baby and Harriet walked into the sea, yearning to get to the boys. 'Hold it, Harriet.' With a soft curse Alice held the baby with one arm and used the other to grab Harriet and hold her back. 'Just wait. They're fine now. Nothing's going to happen to them.' Providing the coastguard managed to pick up the second child and Gio before the tide finally closed over the rapidly vanishing sand spit.

Discovering new depths of tension within herself, Alice watched helplessly as the winchman guided the first child safely into the helicopter and then went down for the second.

By now Gio's feet were underwater and he was

holding the child high in his arms, safely away from the dangerous lick of the sea.

The helicopter held its position, the crowd on the beach grew and there was a communal sigh of relief as the winchman picked up the second child, attached the harness and then guided him safely into the helicopter.

'Oh, thank God!' Harriet burst into tears, her hands over her face. 'Now what?' She turned to Alice. 'Where are they taking them?'

'They'll check them over just in case they need medical help,' Alice told her, her eyes fixed on Gio who was now up to mid-thigh in swirling water. She raked fingers through her hair and clamped her teeth on her lower lip to prevent herself from crying out a warning. What was the point of crying out a warning when the guy could see perfectly well for himself what was happening?

'Will they take them to the hospital?' Harriet was staring up at the helicopter but Alice had her gaze fixed firmly on Gio.

There was no way he'd be able to swim safely now. The water was too deep and the current was just too fierce.

The crowd on the beach must have realised it too because a sudden silence fell as they waited for the helicopter to lower the winchman for a third time.

And finally Harriet saw…

'He's risking his life.' She said the words in hushed tones, as if she'd only just realised what was truly happening. 'Oh, my God, he's risking his life for my babies. And now he's going to—'

'No, he isn't.' Alice snapped the words, refusing to allow her to voice what everyone was thinking. 'He's going to be fine, Harriet,' she said, as much to convince herself as the woman standing next to her in a serious state of anxiety. 'They're lowering the winchman again.'

What was the Italian for *you stupid, brave idiot?* she wondered as she watched Gio exchange a few words with the winchman and then laugh as the harness was attached. They rose up in the air, swinging slightly as they approached the hovering helicopter.

Alice closed her eyes briefly as he vanished inside. For a moment she just felt like sinking onto the sand and staying there until the panic subsided. Then her mobile phone rang. She answered it immediately. It was Gio.

'Twins seem fine but they're taking them to hospital for a quick check.' His voice crackled. 'Tell Harriet I'll bring them home. It isn't safe for her to drive in a state of anxiety and shock and by the time she gets up to the house, picks up the car and drives to the hospital, I'll be home with them.'

Deciding that it wasn't the right moment to yell at him, she simply acknowledged what he'd said and ended the call. 'They seem fine but they're going to take them to the hospital for a check. Dr Moretti will bring them home, Harriet,' she said quietly. 'Let's go back to your house now and make a cup of tea. I don't know about you, but I need one.'

Gio arrived back at the house three hours later. Three long hours during which she'd had all too much time to think about *that kiss* and the fact that she'd told him far more about herself than she'd intended.

Annoyed with herself, confused, Alice abandoned all pretence of reading a medical journal and was pacing backwards and forwards in the kitchen, staring at the clock, when she finally heard the doorbell. She closed her eyes and breathed a sigh of relief.

She opened the door and lifted an eyebrow, trying to regain some of her old self. Trying to react the way she would have reacted before *that kiss*. 'Forgot your key?'

He was wearing a set of theatre scrubs and he looked broad-shouldered and more handsome than a man had a right to look. She sneaked a look at his firm mouth and immediately felt a sizzle in her veins.

'Careless, I know. I went swimming and I must have them in my trousers.' He strolled past her with a lazy grin and pushed the door closed behind him. Suddenly her hallway seemed small.

'Talking of swimming…' she took a step backwards and kept her tone light '…you certainly go to extreme lengths to pull the women, Dr Moretti. Plunging into the jaws of death and acting like a hero. Does it work for you?'

He paused, his eyes on hers, his expression thoughtful. 'I don't know. Let's find out, shall we?' Without warning, he reached out a hand and jerked her against him, his mouth hovering a mere breath from hers. 'We have unfinished business, Dr Anderson.'

He kissed her hard and she felt her knees go weak but she didn't have the chance to think about the implications of that fact because something hot and dangerous exploded in her body. She wound her arms round his neck for support. *Just for support*.

He gave a low groan and dug his fingers into her hair, tilting her head, changing the angle, helping himself to her mouth.

'You taste good, *cara mia*,' he muttered, trailing kisses

over her jaw and then back to her mouth. He kissed her thoroughly. Skilfully. And then lifted his head, his breathing less than steady. 'I'm addicted to your mouth. It was one of the first things I noticed about you.'

Her head swam dizzily and she tried to focus, but before she could even remember how to regain control he lowered his head again.

With a soft gasp, she tried to speak. 'Stop…' His lips had found a sensitive spot on her neck and she was finding it impossible to think straight. With a determined effort, she pushed at his chest. 'We have to stop this.'

'Why?' His mouth returned to hers, teasing and seducing. 'Why stop something that feels so good?'

Her head was swimming and she couldn't concentrate. 'Because I don't do this.'

'Then it's good to try something new.' He lifted his head, his smile surprisingly gentle. 'Courage, *tesoro*.'

Her fingers were curled into the hard muscle of his shoulders and she remembered the strength he'd shown in the water.

'Talking of courage, you could have drowned out there.'

His eyes searched hers. Questioning. 'You're telling me you were worried, Dr Anderson?' He lifted a hand and gently brushed her cheek. 'Better not let Mary hear you say that. She'll be buying a hat to wear at our wedding.'

'Oh, for goodness' sake.' She knew he was teasing but all the same the words flustered her and she pulled away, trying not to look at his mouth. Trying not to think about the way he kissed. About the fact that she wanted him to go on kissing her. 'What took you so long, anyway? I was beginning to think you'd gone back to Italy.'

'I hurried the twins through A and E, we got a ride home with one of the paramedics and then I dropped them home.'

'And that took three hours? Did you drive via Scotland?'

'You really were worried. Careful, Alice.' His voice was soft, his gaze searching. 'You're showing emotion.'

She flushed and walked past him to the kitchen. 'Given the distance between here and the hospital, with which I'm entirely familiar, I was expecting you back ages ago. And you didn't answer your mobile.'

'I was with Harriet.' He followed her and went straight to the espresso machine. 'She had a nasty shock and she was blaming herself terribly for what happened. She needed TLC.'

And he would have given her the comfort she needed, because he was that sort of man. He was good with people's emotions, she thought to herself. Unlike her.

'I stayed with her for the first two hours,' she muttered, raking fingers through her hair, feeling totally inadequate, 'but she just kept pacing and saying she was a terrible mother. And I didn't know what to say. I'm hopeless at giving emotional comfort. If she'd cut her finger or developed a rash, I would have been fine. But there was nothing to see. She was just hysterical and miserable. I did my best, but it wasn't good enough. I was useless.'

He glanced over his shoulder, his eyes gentle. 'That's not true. You're not hopeless or useless. Just a little afraid, I think. Emotions can be scary things. Not so easily explained as some other things. You'll get better with practice. She's calmer now.' Reaching across the work surface, Gio opened a packet of coffee-beans and tipped them into a grinder. 'And she definitely has post-natal depression.'

Alice stared. 'You're sure?'

'Certain.'

'So what did you do?'

'I listened.' He flicked a switch, paused while the beans were ground and then gave a shrug. 'Sometimes that's all a person needs, although, in Harriet's case, I think she does need something more. Tomorrow she is coming to see me and we are going to put together a plan of action. I think her condition merits drug treatment but, more importantly, we need to get her emotional support. Her husband isn't around much and she needs help. She needs to feel that people love and care for her. She needs to know that people mind how she's feeling. She doesn't have family to do that, so we need to find her the support from elsewhere.'

Alice watched him. He moved around the kitchen the same way he did everything. With strength and confidence. 'You really believe that family holds all the answers, don't you?'

'Yes, I do.' He emptied the grinder and turned to look at her. 'But I realise that you may find that hard to understand, given your experience of family life. You haven't ever seen a decent example, so why would you agree with me?'

She stiffened. 'Look, I wish I'd never mentioned it to you. It isn't important.'

'It's stopped you believing in love, so it's important.'

'I don't want to talk about it.'

'That's just because you're not used to talking about

it. A bit like kissing. You'll be fine once you've had more practice.'

The mere mention of kissing made her body heat. 'I don't want more practice! I hate talking about it!'

'Because it stirs up emotions and you're afraid of emotions. Plenty of people have problems in their past, but it doesn't have to affect the future. Only if you let it. Family is perhaps the most important thing in the world, after good health.' His voice was calm as he started making the coffee, his movements steady and methodical. It seemed to her as she watched that making coffee was almost a form of relaxation for him.

'Is that how it happens in Italy? I mean Sicily?' She corrected herself quickly and saw him smile.

'In Sicily, family is sacred.' He watched as coffee trickled into the cup, dark and fragrant. 'We believe in love, Alice. We believe in a love that is special, unique and lasts for a lifetime. I'm surrounded by generations of my family and extended family who have been in love for ever. Come with me to Sicily and I will prove it to you.'

He was teasing, of course. He had to be teasing. 'Don't be ridiculous.'

'You have been to Sicily?' She shook her head and took the coffee he handed to her.

'No.'

His smile was lazy and impossibly attractive. 'It is a land designed to make people believe in romance and passion. We have the glittering sea to seduce, and the fires of Etna to flame the coldest heart.' He spoke in a soft, accented drawl and she rolled her eyes to hide how strongly his words affected her.

'Drop the sweet talk. It's wasted on me, Dr Moretti. Romance is just a seduction tool.'

And she'd had three long hours to think about seduction.

Three long hours to think about the kiss on the beach.

And the way he'd plunged into the water after two small children in trouble.

And now she also had to think about the way he'd spent his evening with a vulnerable, lonely mother with postnatal depression.

Bother.

She was really starting to like the man. And notice things about him. Things that other women probably noticed immediately. Like his easy, slightly teasing smile and the thick, dark lashes that gave his eyes a sleepy look. A dangerous look. The way, when he talked to a woman, he gave her his whole attention. His rich, sexy accent and the smooth, confident way that he dealt with every problem. And the way he shouldered those problems without walking away.

It was just the kiss, she told herself crossly as she drank her coffee. The kiss had made her loopy. Up until then she really hadn't looked at him in *that way*.

'Did you pick up my clothes?' He strolled over to her and she found herself staring at his shoulders. He had good shoulders.

'Sorry?'

'My clothes.' He lifted an eyebrow, his eyes scanning her face. 'Did you pick them up from the beach?'

'Oh.' She pulled herself together and dragged her eyes away from the tangle of dark hairs at the base of his throat. 'Yes. Yes, I did. I put them on the chair in your room.'

Heat curled low in her pelvis and spread through her limbs. Sexual awareness, she told herself. The attraction of female to male. Without it, the human race would have died out. It was a perfectly normal chemical reaction. *It's just that it wasn't normal for her.* She tried to shut the feeling down. Tried to control it. But it was on the loose.

'Thanks.' He was watching her. 'It would have been hard to explain that to Mary if some helpful bystander had delivered them to the surgery tomorrow.'

She folded her arms across her chest in a defensive gesture. 'It would have made Mary's day.'

'So would this, I suspect.' He lowered his head and kissed her again, his mouth lingering on hers.

This time she didn't even think about resisting. She just closed her eyes and let herself feel. Allowed the heat to spread through her starving body. Her nerves sang and hummed and when he finally lifted his head she felt only disappointment.

It was amazing how quickly a person could adapt to being touched, she thought dizzily.

'I—We…' She lifted a hand to her lips and then let it drop back to her side, suddenly self-conscious. 'You've got to stop doing that.' But even she knew the words were a lie and he gave a smile as he walked towards the door.

'I'm going to keep doing it, *cara mia.*' He turned in the doorway. Paused. His eyes burned into hers. 'So you're just going to have to get used to it.'

CHAPTER EIGHT

GIO looked at Harriet and felt his heart twist. She looked so utterly miserable.

'Crazy, isn't it?' Her voice was little more than a whisper. 'I have this beautiful, perfect baby and I'm not even enjoying having her. I snap at the twins and yesterday I was so miserable I didn't even notice that they'd wandered off.'

'Don't be so hard on yourself and never underestimate a child's capacity for mischief,' Gio said calmly. 'They are young and adventurous, as small boys should be.'

'But I can't cope with them. I'm just so tired.' Her eyes filled. 'I snap at Geoff and he says that suddenly he's married to a witch, and I really can't face sex…' She blushed, her expression embarrassed. 'Sorry, I didn't mean to say that. Geoff would kill me if he thought I was talking about our sex life in the village.'

'This isn't the village,' Gio said gently. 'It's my consulting room and I'm a doctor. And it's important that you tell me everything you are feeling so that I can make an informed judgement on how to help you.'

Her eyes filled and she clamped a hand over her mouth, struggling for control. 'I'm sorry to be so pathetic, it's just that I'm so tired. I'll be fine when I've had some sleep—the trouble is I don't get any. I'm so tired I ought to go out like a light but I can't sleep at all and I'm totally on edge all the time. I'm an absolutely *terrible* mother. And do you know the worst thing?' Giving up her attempts at control, she burst into heartbreaking sobs. Gio reached across his desk for a box of tissues, his eyes never leaving her face.

'Tell me.'

'I'm so useless I don't even know what my own baby wants.' Wrenching a tissue from the box, she blew her nose hard. 'She's my third child and I find myself sitting there, staring at her while she's crying, totally unable to move. And I worry about everything. I worry I'm going to go to her cot in the morning and find she's died in the night, I worry that she's going to catch something awful and I won't notice—'

Gio put his hand over hers. 'You're describing symptoms of anxiety, Harriet, and I think—'

'You think that I'm basically a completely terrible mother and a hideously pathetic blubbery female.' She blew her nose again and he shook his head and tightened his grip on her hand.

'On the contrary, I think you are a wonderful mother.' He hesitated, choosing his words carefully. 'But I think it's possible that you could be suffering from depression.'

She frowned. Dropped the tissue into her bag. 'I'm just tired.'

'I don't think so.' He kept his hand on hers and she clamped her lower lip between her teeth, trying not to cry.

'I can't be depressed. Oh, God, I just need to pull myself together.'

'Depression is an illness. It isn't about pulling yourself together.'

Her eyes filled again and she reached for another tissue. 'Do you mean depressed as in postnatal depression?'

'Yes, that's exactly what I think.'

Tears trickled down her face. 'So maybe this isn't just about me being useless?'

'You're not useless. In fact, I think the opposite.' He shook his head, a look of admiration on his face. 'How you are coping with three children under the age of six and postnatal depression, I just don't know.'

'I'm not coping.'

'Yes, you are. Just not as well as you'd like. And you're not enjoying yourself.' Gio let go of her hand and turned back to his desk, reaching for a pad of paper. 'But that's going to change, Harriet. We're going to sort this out for you.'

She blew her nose. 'My husband will just tell me to pull myself together and snap out of it.'

'He won't say that,' Gio scribbled on a pad, 'because I'm going to talk to him. Many people are ignorant about the true nature of postnatal depression, he isn't alone in that. Once I explain everything to him, he will give you the support you need. I've spoken to Gina, the health visitor, and done some research. This is a group that I think you might find helpful.' He handed her the piece of paper and she looked at it.

'It's only in the next village.'

Gio nodded. 'Will you be able to get there?'

'Oh, yes. I can drive.' She stared at the name. 'Do I have to phone?'

'I've done it. They're expecting you at their next

meeting, which happens to be tomorrow afternoon. You can take the twins and the baby, there'll be someone there to help.'

Harriet looked at him. 'Do I need drugs?'

'I'd like to try talking therapy first and I want to see you regularly. If you don't start to feel better then drug treatment might be appropriate. Let's see how we go.'

Harriet slipped the paper into her bag and gave a feeble smile. 'I feel a bit better already, just knowing that this isn't all my fault.'

'None of it is your fault.' Gio rose to his feet and walked her to the door. 'Go to the meeting and let me know how you get on.'

Alice parked her newly fixed car outside her house and stared at the low black sports car that meant that Gio was already back from his house calls.

Bother. She'd been hoping that he'd work late.

It had been almost a week since the episode on the beach. A week during which she'd virtually lived in the surgery in order to put some distance between her and Gio. A week during which she'd drunk endless cups of black coffee and eaten nothing but sandwiches at her desk. A week during which she'd been cranky and thoroughly unsettled. It was as if her neat, tidy life had been thrown into the air and had landed in a different pattern. And she didn't know how to put it back together.

What she did know was that it was Gio's fault for kissing her.

And Mary's fault for arranging for him to lodge with her.

Pushing open the front door, she was stopped by the smell.

'Well, well. The wanderer returns. I was beginning to think you'd taken root in the surgery.' Gio emerged from the kitchen and her heart stumbled and jerked. A pair of old, faded jeans hugged his hard thighs and his black shirt was open at the neck. 'If you hadn't returned home at a decent hour, I was coming to find you.'

Even dressed so casually he looked handsome and—she searched for the word—exotic?

'I had work to do. And now I'm tired.' She had to escape. Had to get her mind back together. 'I'm going straight up to bed, if you don't mind.'

'Alice.' His tone was gentle and there was humour in his eyes. 'It's not even eight o'clock, *tesoro*. If you are going to try and avoid me, you're going to have to think of a better excuse than that. You've kept your distance for a week. It's long enough, I think.'

Something in his tone stung. He made her feel like a coward. 'Why would I try and avoid you?'

'Because I make you uncomfortable. I make you talk when you'd rather be silent and I make you feel when you'd rather stay numb.'

'I don't—'

'And because I kissed you and made you want something that you've made a point of denying yourself for years.'

'I don't—'

'At least eat with me.' He held out a hand. 'And if after that you want to go to bed, I'll let you go.'

She kept her hands by her sides. 'You've cooked?'

'I like cooking. I've made a Sicilian speciality. It's

too much for one person and, anyway, I need your opinion.' His hand remained outstretched and there was challenge in his dark eyes.

Muttering under her breath about bullying Italian men, she took his hand and felt his strong fingers close firmly over hers.

Instead of leading her into the kitchen, he took her into the dining room. The dining room at the back of the house that she never used. The dining room that was now transformed.

All the clutter was gone and tiny candles flickered on every available surface. The smells of a warm summer evening drifted in through the open French doors.

The atmosphere was intimate. Romantic.

Something flickered inside her. Panic? She turned to him with a shake of her head. 'No, Gio. This isn't what I do, I—'

He covered her lips with his fingers. 'Relax, *tesoro*. It's just dinner. Food is always more enjoyable when the atmosphere is good, and the atmosphere in this room is perfect. Go and take a shower and change. Dinner is in fifteen minutes.'

She stared after him as he strolled back to the kitchen. The guy just couldn't help himself. He'd obviously decided that she needed rescuing from her past and he thought he was the one to do it. The one to show her that romance existed.

She stared at the candles and rolled her eyes. Well, if he thought that a few lumps of burning wax were going to make her fall in love, he was doomed to disappointment.

Telling herself that she was only doing it because she was hot and uncomfortable, she showered and changed into a simple white strap top and a green silk skirt that hugged her hips softly and then fell to mid-thigh.

Staring at her reflection in the mirror, she contemplated make-up and decided against it. She didn't want to look as though she was making an effort. She didn't want him getting the wrong idea.

With that thought on her mind, she walked back into the dining room and came straight to the point.

'I know that some women would just drop to their knees and beg for a man who does all this.' She waved a hand around the room. 'But I'm not one of them. Really. I'm happy with a sandwich eaten under a halogen light bulb. So if you're trying to make me fall in love with you, you're wasting your time. I just thought we ought to get that straight right now, before you go to enormous effort.'

'I'm not trying to make you fall in love with me. True love can't be forced,' he said softly as he pulled the cork out of a bottle of wine, 'and it can't be commanded. True love is a gift, *cara mia*. Freely given by both parties.'

'It's a figment of the imagination. A serious hallucination,' she returned, her tone sharper than she'd intended. 'A justification for wild, impulsive and totally irrational behaviour, usually between two people who are old enough to know better.'

'That isn't love.' He pushed her towards the chair that faced the window. 'From what you've told me, you haven't seen an example of love. But you will do. I intend to show you.'

She rolled her eyes and watched while he filled her glass. 'What are you? My fairy godmother?'

His smile broadened. 'Do I look like a fairy to you?'

She swallowed hard and dragged her eyes away from the laughter in his. No. He looked like a thoroughly gorgeous man. And he was standing in her dining room about to serve her dinner.

'All right.' She gave a shrug that she hoped looked suitably casual. 'I'm hungry. Let's agree to disagree and just eat.'

The food was delicious.

Never in her life had she ever tasted anything so sublime. And through it all Gio topped up her wineglass and kept up a neutral conversation. He was intelligent and entertaining and she forgot her plan to eat as fast as possible and then escape to her room. Instead she ate, savouring every mouthful, and sipped her wine. And all the time she listened as he talked.

He talked about growing up on Sicily and about his life as a surgeon in Milan. He talked about the differences in medicine between the two cultures.

'So…' She reached for more bread. 'Are you going to tell me why you had to give up surgery as a career? Or am I the only one who has to spill about my past?'

'It's not a secret.' He lounged across the table from her, his face bronzed and handsome in the flickering candlelight. 'I was working in Africa. We were attacked by rebels hoping to steal drugs and equipment that they could sell on.' He gave a shrug and lifted his glass. 'Unfortunately the damage was such that I can't operate for any length of time.'

She winced. 'I'm sorry, I shouldn't have asked.'

'It's part of my life and talking about it doesn't make it worse. In a way I was lucky. I took some time off and went home to my family.' He continued to talk, telling her about his sisters and his brother, his parents, his grandparents and numerous aunts, uncles and cousins.

'You were lucky.' She put her glass down on the table. 'Having such good family.'

'Yes, I was.' He passed her more bread. 'Luckier than you.'

'She took me to the park once—my mother.' She stared at her plate, the memory rising into her brain so clearly that her hands curled into fists and her shoulders tensed. 'She was meeting her lover and I was the excuse that enabled her to leave the house without my dad suspecting anything. Although I doubt he would have cared because he was seeing someone, too. Only she didn't know that.'

She looked up, waiting for him to display shock or distaste, but Gio sat still, his eyes on her face. Listening. It occurred to her that he was an excellent listener.

She shrugged. 'Anyway, I was playing on the climbing frame. They were sitting on the seat. Kissing. Wrapped up in each other.' She licked dry lips. 'I remember watching two other children and envying them. Their mothers were both hovering at the bottom of the climbing frame, hands outstretched. They said things like "be careful" and "watch where you put your feet" and "that's too high, come down now". My mother didn't even glance in my direction.' She broke off and ran a hand over the back of her neck, the tension rising inside her. 'Not even when I fell. And in the ambulance she was furious with me and accused me of sabotaging her relationship on purpose.'

Gio reached across the table and took her hand. But still he didn't speak. Just listened, his eyes holding hers.

She chewed her lip and flashed him a smile. 'Anyway, he was husband number two and life just carried on from there, really. She went through two more— Oh, sorry.' She gave a cynical smile that was loaded with pain. 'I should say she "fell in love" twice more before I was finally old enough to leave home.'

'And your sister?'

Alice rubbed her fingers over her forehead. 'She's on her second marriage. She had high hopes of doing everything differently to our parents. She still believed that true love existed. I think she's finally discovering that it doesn't. I've never told anyone any of this before. Not even Rita and Mary. They know I'm not in touch with my parents, but that's all they know.'

It had grown dark while she was talking and through the open doors she could hear the sounds of the night, see the flutter of insects drawn by the flickering candlelight.

Finally Gio spoke. 'It's not surprising that you don't believe that love exists. It's hard to believe in something that you've never seen. You have a logical, scientific brain, Alice. You take a problem-solving approach to life. Love is not easily defined or explained and that makes it easy to dismiss.'

She swallowed. How was it that he seemed to understand her so well? And why had she just told him so much? She looked suspiciously at her wineglass but it was still half-full and her head was clear. She waited for regret to flood through her but instead she felt strangely peaceful for the first time. 'If love really existed then the divorce rate wouldn't be so high.'

'Or maybe love just isn't that easy to find, and that

makes it even more precious. Maybe the divorce rate is testament to the fact that love is so special that people are willing to take a risk in order to find it.'

She shook her head. 'What people feel is sexual chemistry and, if they're lucky, friendship. But there isn't a whole separate emotion called love that binds people together.'

'Because you haven't seen it yet.' He studied her face. 'True love is selfless and yet the emotion you saw was greedy and selfish. They allowed you to fall and they weren't there to catch you.'

Instinctively she knew he wasn't just talking about the incident on the climbing frame.

She lifted her glass. 'So, if you believe in love, Dr Moretti, why aren't you married with eight children?' Her eyes challenged him over the rim of her glass and he smiled.

'Because you don't choose when to love. Or even who to love. You can't just go out and find it in the way that you can find friendship or sex. Love chooses you. And chooses the time. For some people it's early in life. For others…' he gave a shrug that showed his Latin heritage '…it's later.'

She frowned. 'So you're waiting for Signorina Right to just bang on your door?' Her tone had a hint of sarcasm and he smiled.

'No. She gave me a key.' Something in his gaze made her heart stop.

Surely he wasn't saying…

He couldn't be suggesting…

She put her glass down. 'Gio—'

'Go to bed, *tesoro*,' he said softly. 'The other thing

about love is that it can't be controlled. Not the emotion and not the timing. It happens when it happens.'

She stared at him. 'But—'

He rose to his feet and smiled. 'Sleep well, Alice.'

Gio left via the back door, knowing that if he didn't leave the house, he'd join her in her bedroom.

It had taken every ounce of willpower to let her walk away from him.

But he knew instinctively that they'd taken enough steps forward for one night. She'd talked—really talked—perhaps for the first time in her life and he could tell that she was starting to relax around him.

Which was how he wanted it to be.

They'd come a long way in a short time.

He breathed in the warm, evening air and strolled down towards the sea, enjoying the comfort of the semi-darkness.

It felt strange, he thought to himself as he walked, to have fallen in love with a woman who didn't even believe that love existed.

After that night, the evenings developed a pattern and, almost a month after he'd arrived in the surgery, Alice sat staring out of the window of her consulting room, wondering what Gio would be cooking for dinner.

It was so unlike her to dream about food, but since he'd taken over the cooking she found herself looking forward to the evenings.

Sometimes they ate in the dining room, sometimes they ate in her garden and once he'd made a picnic and they'd taken it down to the beach.

Thinking, dreaming, she missed the tap on the door.

It was friendship, she decided, and she liked it.

She could really talk to him and he was an excellent listener. And she enjoyed working with him. He was an excellent doctor.

And, of course, there was sexual chemistry. She wasn't so naïve that she couldn't recognise it. She'd even experienced it before, to a lesser degree, with a man she'd dated a few times at university. Not love, but a chemical reaction between a man and a woman. And it was there, between her and Gio.

But since the incident on the beach, he hadn't kissed her again.

Hadn't made any attempt to touch her.

The door behind her opened. 'Alice?'

Why hadn't he touched her since?

'Dr Anderson?'

Finally she heard her name, and turned to find Mary standing in the doorway. 'Are you on our planet?'

'Just thinking.'

'Dreaming, you mean.' Mary looked at her curiously and then handed her a set of notes. 'You've got one extra. The little Jarrett boy has a high temperature. I don't like the look of him so I squeezed him in.'

'That's fine, Mary.' She took the notes. 'Thanks.'

She pulled herself together, saw Tom Jarrett and then walked through to Reception with the notes just as Gio emerged from his consulting room, with his hand on Edith Carne's shoulder.

He was so tactile, Alice thought to herself, observing the way he guided the woman up the corridor, his head tilted towards her as he listened.

Touching came entirely naturally to him, whereas she—

'The cardiology referral was a good idea,' he said to her as he strolled back from reception and saw her watching him. 'They're treating Edith and it appears that they've found the cause of her falls.'

'You mean, you found the cause. She never would have—'

A series of loud screams from Reception interrupted her and she exchanged a quick glance with Gio before hurrying to the reception area just as a mother came struggled through the door, carrying a sobbing child. He was screaming and crying and holding his foot.

Alice stepped towards them. 'What's happened?'

'I don't know. We were on the beach and then suddenly he just started screaming for no reason.' The mother was breathless from her sprint from the beach and the child continued to howl noisily. 'His foot is really red and it's swelling up.'

Gio picked up the foot and examined it. 'Erythema. Oedema. A sting of some sort?'

Alice tilted her head and looked. 'Weaver fish,' she said immediately, and glanced towards Mary. 'Get me hot water, please. Fast.'

Mary nodded and Gio frowned. 'What?'

'If you're expecting the Italian translation you're going to be waiting a long time,' Alice drawled, her fingers gentle as she examined the child's foot, 'but basically weaver fish are found in sandy shallows around the beaches down here. It has venomous spines on its dorsal fin and that protrudes out of the sand. If you tread on it, you get stung.'

The mother shook her head. 'I didn't see anything on the sand.'

'It's a good idea to keep something on your feet when you're walking in the shallows at low water,' Alice advised, taking the bucket of water that Mary handed her with a nod of thanks. 'All right, sweetheart, we're going to put your foot in this water and that will help the pain.'

She tested the water quickly to check that it wasn't so hot that it would burn the child and then tried to guide the child's foot into the water. He jerked his leg away and his screams intensified.

'We really have to get this into hot water.' Alice looked at the mother. 'Heat inactivates the venom. After a few minutes in here, the pain will be better. Trust me.'

'Alex, please…' the mother begged, and tried to reason with her son. 'You need to put your foot in the bucket for Mummy. Please, darling, do it for Mummy.'

Alex continued to yell and bawl and wriggle and Gio rubbed a hand over his roughened jaw and crouched down. 'We play a game,' he said firmly, sounding more Italian than ever. He produced a penny from his pocket, held it up and then promptly made it disappear.

Briefly, Alex stopped crying and stared. 'Where?'

Gio looked baffled. 'I don't know. Perhaps if you put your foot in the bucket, it will reappear. Like magic. Let's try it, shall we?'

Alex sniffed, hesitated and then tentatively dipped his foot in the water. 'It's hot.'

'It has to be hot,' Alice said quickly, guiding his foot into the water. 'It will take the pain away.'

She watched gratefully as Gio distracted Alex, producing the coin from behind the child's ear and then from his own ear.

Alex watched, transfixed, and Gio treated him to ten minutes of magic, during which time the child's misery lessened along with the pain.

'Oh, thank goodness,' the mother said, as Alex finally started smiling. 'That was awful. And I had no idea. I've never even heard of a weaver fish.'

'They're not uncommon. There were five hundred cases along the North Devon and Cornwall coast last year,' Alice muttered as she dried her hands on the towel that Mary had thought to provide. 'Keep his foot in the bucket for another ten minutes at least and give him some paracetamol and antihistamine when you get home. He should be fine but if he isn't, give us a call.'

'Thank you so much.' The mother looked at her gratefully. 'What would I have done if you'd been shut?'

'Actually, lots of the cafés and surf shops around here keep a bucket just for this purpose so it's worth re-membering that. But the best advice is to avoid walking near the low-water mark in bare feet.'

Alice walked over to the reception desk and Gio followed.

'Weaver fish? What is this weaver fish?' He spoke slowly, as if he wasn't sure he was pronouncing it correctly.

'Nobody knows exactly what is in weaver fish venom but it contains a mixture of biogenous amines and they've identified 5-hydroxytryptamine, epinephrine, norepinephrine and histamine.' She angled her head. 'Alex was probably stung by *Echiichthys vipera*—the lesser weaver fish.'

Gio lifted a brow. 'Implying that there is a greater weaver fish?'

She nodded. '*Trachinus draco*. There are case reports of people being stung. Often fisherman. We've seen one in this practice. It was a few years ago, but we sent him up to the hospital to be treated. The symptoms are severe pain, vomiting, oedema, syncope—in his case, the symptoms lasted for a long time.'

He smiled at her and she frowned, her heart beating faster as she looked into his eyes.

'What? Why are you looking at me like that?'

'Because I love it when you give me facts.' He leaned closer to her, his eyes dancing. 'You are delightfully serious, Dr Anderson, do you know that? And I find you incredibly sexy.'

'Gio, for goodness' sake.' Her eyes slid towards Mary, who was filling out a form with the mother. But she couldn't drench the flame of desire that burned through her body.

And he saw that flame.

'We're finished here.' Gio's voice was low and determined. 'Let's go home, Dr Anderson.'

'But—'

'It's home, or it's your consulting room with the door locked. Take your pick.'

She chose home.

CHAPTER NINE

THEY barely made it through the front door.

The tension that had been building for weeks reached breaking point as she fumbled with her key in the lock, aware that he was right behind her, his hand resting on the small of her back.

Gio's fingers closed over hers and guided. Turned the key. And then he was nudging her inside and shouldering the door closed.

For a moment they both stood, breathing heavily, poised on the edge of something dangerous.

And then they cracked. Both moved at the same time, mouths greedy, hands seeking.

'I need you naked.' He ripped at Alice's shirt, sending buttons flying across the floor, and she reciprocated, fumbling with his buttons while her breath came in tiny pants.

'Me, too. Me, too.' And all the time a tiny voice in her head was telling her that she didn't do this sort of thing.

She ignored it and slipped his shirt from his shoulders, revelling in the feel of warm male flesh under her hands. 'You have a perfect body, Dr Moretti.'

He gave a groan and slid his hands up her back, his

eyes feasting on the swell of her breasts under her simple lacy bra. He spoke softly in Italian and then scooped her into his arms and carried her up the stairs to her bedroom.

'I don't understand a word you're saying, but I suppose it might be better that way. I like it.' With a tiny laugh she buried her head in his neck, breathed in the tantalising scent of aroused male and then murmured in protest as he lowered her onto the bed. 'I want you to carry on holding me. Don't let me go.'

'No chance.' With a swift movement he removed his trousers and came down on top of her, his hands sliding into her hair, his mouth descending to hers. 'And this from the girl who hated being touched.'

He was touching her now. Everywhere. His hands seeking, seducing, soothing all at the same time.

'That was before—' She arched under him, burning to get closer still to his hard, male body while his hands explored ever curve of hers. 'Before…'

'Before?' His hand slid over her breast and she realised in a daze that she hadn't even felt him remove her bra.

'Before you.' The flick of his tongue over her nipple brought a gasp to her throat and she curled a leg around him, the ache in her pelvis intensifying to unbearable proportions. 'Before I met you.' The touch of his mouth was skilful and sinful in equal measures and she closed her eyes and felt the erotic pull deep in her stomach.

'You're beautiful.' His mouth trailed lower and his fingers dragged at her tiny panties, sliding them downwards, leaving her naked.

She slid a hand over the hard planes of his chest, felt his touch grow more intimate. His fingers moved over her, then his mouth, and she offered herself freely, wondering what had happened to her inhibitions.

Drowning in sensation, she shifted and gasped and finally he rose over her and she reached for him, desperate.

'Now.' Her eyes were fevered and her lips were parted. 'I need you now. Now.'

And he gathered her against him and took her, his possessive thrust bringing a gasp to her lips and a flush to her cheeks. For a moment he stilled, his eyes locked on hers, his breathing unsteady. And then he lowered his head and his mouth covered hers in a kiss that was hot and demanding, his powerful body moving against hers in a rhythm that created sensations so exquisitely perfect that she cried out in desperation.

Her skin was damp from the heat and her fingers raked his back as the sensation built and threatened to devour her whole.

She toppled fast, falling into a dark void of ecstasy, and immediately he slowed the pace, changing the rhythm from desperate to measured, always the one in control.

With a low moan she opened her eyes and slid her arms round his neck. 'What are you doing?'

'Making love to you.' He spoke the words against her lips, the hot brand of his mouth sending her senses tumbling in every direction. 'And I don't ever want to stop.'

She didn't want him to stop either and she arched her back and moved her hips until she felt the change in him. Felt his muscles quiver and his skin grow slick, heard the rasp of his breath and the increase in masculine thrust.

And then she felt nothing more because he drove them both forward until they reached oblivion and fell, tumbling and gasping into a whirlpool of sexual excitement that sucked them both under.

She lay there, eyes closed, struggling for breath and sanity. His weight should have bothered her, but it didn't.

And she was relieved that he didn't seem able to move either.

Eventually he lifted his head and nuzzled her neck gently, his movements slow and languid. 'Are we still alive?' With a fractured groan he rolled onto his back, taking her with him. 'You need to wear more clothes around the house. I find it hard to resist you when you're naked.'

Her eyes were still closed. 'It's your fault that I'm naked.'

'It is?' He stroked her hair away from her face and something about the way he was touching her made her open her eyes. And she saw.

'Gio—'

'I love you, Alice.'

Her heart jerked. Jumped. Kick-started by pure, blind panic. 'No need to get all mushy on me, Dr Moretti. You already scored.'

'That's why I'm saying it now. If I'd said it when we were making love then you would have thought it was just the heat of the moment. If I said it over dinner with candles and wine, you would have said it was the romance of the moment. So I'm saying it now. After we've made love. Because that's what we just did.'

'I don't need to hear this.' She tried to wriggle away from him but he held her easily, his powerful body trapping hers.

'Yes, you do. The problem is that you're not used to

hearing it. But that's going to change because I'm going to be saying it to you a lot. A few weeks ago you weren't used to talking or touching but you do both those now.'

'This is different.' Her heart was pounding. 'It was just sex, Gio. Great sex, admittedly, but nothing more.'

His mouth trailed over her breast and she groaned and tried to push him away. 'Stop. You're not playing fair.'

'I'm in love with you. And I'm just reminding you how you feel about me.' He lifted his head, a wicked smile in his eyes, and she ran a hand over her shoulder, trying not to lick her lips. He had an incredible body and every female part of her craved him.

But that was natural, she reminded herself. 'It's sexual attraction,' she said hoarsely, trying to concentrate despite the skilled movement of his mouth and hands. 'If sexual attraction didn't exist then the human race would have died out long ago. It isn't love.' She gave a low moan as his fingers teased her intimately. 'Gio…'

'Not love?' He rolled onto his back and positioned her above him. 'Fine, Dr Anderson. Then let's have sex. At the moment I don't care what you call it as long as you stop talking.'

A week later, Alice walked into work with a smile on her face and a bounce in her step.

And she knew why, of course.

It was her relationship with Gio. And she was totally clear about her feelings. Friendship and sex. It was turning out to be a good combination. In a month or so he'd probably be leaving and that would be fine. Maybe they'd stay in touch. Maybe they wouldn't. Either way, she felt fine about it. She felt fine about everything.

And the fact that he always said 'I love you' and she didn't just didn't seem to matter any more. It didn't change the way things were between them.

The truth was, they were having fun.

Mary caught her as she walked into her consulting room. 'You're looking happy.'

'I am happy.' She dropped her bag behind the desk and turned on her computer. 'I'm enjoying my life.'

'You weren't smiling this much a month ago.'

A month ago Gio hadn't been in her life.

She frowned slightly at the thought and then dismissed it. What was wrong with enjoying a friendship?

'Professor Burrows from the haematology department at the hospital rang.' Mary handed her a piece of paper. 'He wants you to call him back on this number before ten o'clock. And I've slotted in Mrs Bruce because she's in a state. She had a scan at the hospital and they think the baby has a cleft palate. She's crying in Reception.'

Alice looked up in concern. 'Oh, poor thing. Send her straight in.' She flicked on her computer while Mary watched, her eyes searching.

'It's Gio, isn't it?'

'What is?'

'The reason you're smiling. So relaxed. You're in love with him, Alice.'

'I'm not in love.' Alice lifted her head and smiled sweetly. 'And the reason I know that is because there's no such thing. But I'm willing to admit that I like him a lot. I respect and admire him as a doctor. He's a nice man.'

And he was great in bed.

Mary looked at her thoughtfully. 'A nice man? Good, I'm glad you like him.'

Alice felt slightly smug as she buzzed for her first patient. Really, in her opinion, it all went to prove that love just didn't exist. In many ways Gio was perfect. He was intelligent and sharp and yet still managed to be kind and thoughtful. He was a terrific listener, a great conversationalist and a spectacular lover. What more could a girl want in a man?

The answer was nothing. But still she didn't feel anything that could be described as love. And when he left to return to Italy, as he inevitably would, she'd miss him but she wouldn't pine.

Which just went to prove that she'd been right all along.

There was a tap on the door and she looked up as Mrs Bruce entered, her face pale and her eyes tired.

'I'm sorry to bother you, Dr Anderson,' she began, but Alice immediately shook her head.

'Don't apologise. I understand you had a scan.'

Mrs Bruce sank into the chair and started to sob quietly. 'And they think the baby has a cleft palate.' The tears poured down her cheeks and she fumbled in her bag for a tissue. 'There was so much I wanted to ask. I had all these questions…' Her voice cracked. 'But the girl couldn't answer any of them and now I have to wait to see some consultant or other and I can't even remember his name.' The sobs became gulps. 'They don't know what it's like. The waiting.'

'It will be Mr Phillips, the consultant plastic surgeon, I expect.' Alice reached for her phone and pressed the button that connected her to Gio's room. 'Dr Moretti?

If you could come into my room for one moment when you've finished with your patient, I'd be grateful.'

Then she replaced the receiver and stood up. 'You poor thing.' She slipped an arm around the woman's shoulders and gave her a hug without even thinking about it. 'You've had a terrible shock. But there's plenty that can be done, trust me. There's an excellent cleft lip and palate team at the hospital. They serve the whole region and I promise that you won't leave this surgery until you know more about what to expect, even if I have to ring the consultant myself.'

Mrs Bruce blew her nose hard and shook her head. 'She isn't even born yet,' she said in a wavering voice, 'and already I'm worried that she's going to be teased and bullied at school. You know what kids are like. They're cruel. And appearance is everything.'

Alice gave her another squeeze and then looked up as Gio walked into the room.

'Dr Moretti—this is Mrs Bruce. The hospital have told her that her baby has a cleft palate and she's terribly upset, which is totally understandable. They don't seem to have given her much information so I thought you might be able to help reassure her about a few things. Answer some questions for her.'

'It's just a shock, you know?' Mrs Bruce clung to Alice's arm like a lifeline and Gio nodded as he pulled out another chair and sat down next to her.

'First let me tell you that I trained as a plastic surgeon,' he said quietly, 'and I specialised in the repair of cleft lips and palates so I know a lot about it.'

Mrs Bruce crumpled the tissue in her hand. 'Why are you a GP, then?'

Gio pulled a face and spread his hands. 'Unfortunately life does not always turn out the way we intend.
I had an accident which meant I could no longer operate
for long periods. So I changed direction in my career.'

'So you've operated on children with this? Can you
make them look normal?'

'In the hands of a skilled surgeon the results can be
excellent but, of course, there are no guarantees and
there are many factors involved. A cleft lip can range in
severity from a slight notch in the red part of the upper
lip…' he gestured with his finger '…to a complete separation of the lip, extending into the nose. The aim of
surgery is to close the separation in the first operation
and to achieve symmetry, but that isn't always possible.'

He was good, Alice thought to herself as she sat
quietly, listening along with the mother. Really good.

Mrs Bruce sniffed. 'Will they do it straight away
when she's born?'

'They usually wait until the baby is ten weeks old.
The repair of a cleft palate requires more extensive surgery and is usually done when the child is between nine
and eighteen months old so that it is better able to
tolerate the procedure.'

'Is it a huge operation?'

'In some children a cleft palate may involve only a
tiny portion at the back of the roof of the mouth or it
might be a complete separation that extends from front
to back.' Gio reached for a pad and a pen that was lying
on Alice's desk. 'It will make more sense if I draw you
a picture.'

Mrs Bruce watched as his pen flew over the page,
demonstrating the defect and the repair. 'How will she

be able to suck if her mouth is—?' She broke off and gave a sniff. 'If her mouth looks like that?'

'There are special bottles that will help her feed.' Gio put the pad down on the desk. 'Looking after the child with a cleft lip and palate has to be a team approach, Mrs Bruce. She may need help with feeding, with speech and other aspects of her development. The surgeon is really only one member of the team. You will have plenty of support, be assured of that.'

Alice sat patiently while Gio talked, reassuring the mother, answering questions and explaining as best he could.

Finally, when she seemed calmer, he reached for the pad again and scribbled a number on a piece of paper. 'If you have other worries, things you think of later and wish you'd asked, you can call me,' he said gently, handing her the piece of paper.

She stared at it. 'You're giving me your phone number?'

He nodded. 'Use it, if you have questions. If the hospital tells you something you don't understand. Or you can always make an appointment, of course.'

'Thank you.' Mrs Bruce gave him a shaky smile and then turned to Alice and squeezed her hand. 'And thank you, too, Dr Anderson.'

'We'll tackle the problem together, Mrs Bruce,' Alice said firmly. 'She'll be managed by the hospital, but never forget that you're still our patient.' She watched Mrs Bruce—a much happier Mrs Bruce—leave the room and then turned to Gio. 'Thanks for that. I didn't have a clue what to say to her. And I don't know much about cleft palates. Will the baby have long-term problems?'

Gio pulled a face. 'Possibly many. They can be very prone to recurrent middle-ear infections, which can lead to scarring of the ossicular chain in the middle ear, and that can damage hearing or even cause deafness.'

'Why are they susceptible to ear infections?'

'In cleft babies, the muscle sling across the palate is incomplete, divided by the cleft, so they can't pull on the eustachian tube,' he explained. 'Also, scar formation following the postnatal correction of cleft lip and palate can lead to abnormal soft tissue, bone and dental growth. There has been some research looking at the possibilities of operating *in utero* in the hope of achieving healing without scarring.'

This was his area. His speciality. And she was fascinated. 'What else?'

'Sometimes there is a gap in the bone, known as the alveolar defect. Then the maxillary facial surgeon will do an alveolar bone graft.'

There was something in his face that made her reach out and touch his arm. 'Do you miss it, Gio?'

'Sometimes.' He gave a lopsided smile. 'Not always.'

'Well, you were great with her. I knew you would be.'

'You were good with her, too.' He shot her a curious look. 'Do you even realise how much you've changed.'

'Changed? How have I changed?' She went back to her chair and hit a button on her computer.

'You were touching a patient and you were doing it instinctively. You were offering physical comfort and emotional support.'

Alice frowned. 'Well, she was upset.'

'Yes.' Gio's voice was soft. 'She was. And you coped well with it. Emotions, Alice. Emotions.'

'What exactly are you implying?'

'That you're getting used to touching and being touched.' He strolled to the door. 'All I have to do now is persuade you to admit that you love me. Tomorrow I'm taking you out to dinner. Prepare yourself.'

'That's nice.' Her breath caught at the look in his eyes. She didn't love him. *She had absolutely nothing to worry about because she didn't love him.* 'Where are we going?'

'My favourite place to eat in the whole world.'

'Oh.' She felt a flicker of surprise. Knowing Gio's tastes for the spectacular, she was surprised that there was anywhere locally that would satisfy him. Perhaps he'd discovered somewhere new. 'I'll look forward to it.'

It took a considerable amount of planning and a certain amount of deviousness on his part, but finally he had it all arranged.

He was gambling everything on a hunch.

The hunch that she loved him but wasn't even aware of it herself.

She'd lived her whole life convinced that love didn't exist, so persuading her to change her mind at this stage wouldn't be easy.

Words alone had failed and so had sexual intimacy, so for days he'd racked his brains for another way of proving to her that love existed. That she could let herself feel what he already knew that she felt.

And finally he'd come up with a plan.

A plan that had involved a considerable number of other people.

And now all he could do was wait. Wait and hope.

* * *

Alice had just finished morning surgery the following day when Gio strolled into the room.

'Fancy a quick lunch?' His tone was casual and she gave a nod, surprised by how eager she was to leave work and spend time with him.

'Why not?' It was just because she enjoyed his company and was making the most of it while he was here. What was wrong with that?

She followed him out of the surgery, expecting him to turn and walk up the street to the coffee-shop. Instead, he turned left, round the back of the building and towards the surgery car park.

'You're taking the car?' She frowned. 'Where are we going?'

'Wait and see.' He held the door of his car open and she slipped into the passenger seat, a question in her eyes.

'We can't go far. We have to be back for two o'clock.'

He covered his eyes with a pair of sunglasses and gave her a smile. 'Stop thinking about work for five minutes.'

It was on the tip of her tongue to tell him that she hardly thought about work at all these days, but something stopped her. If she made a comment like that, he'd read something into it that wasn't there.

Wondering where he could possibly be taking her and thinking that he was acting very strangely, Alice sat back in her seat and pondered some of the problems that she'd seen that morning. And found she couldn't concentrate on any of them.

It was Gio's fault, she thought crossly. Going out for lunch with him was too distracting. She should have said no.

The wind played with her hair and she caught it and swept it out of her eyes. And noticed where they were.

'This is the airport.' She glanced behind her to check that she wasn't mistaken. 'Gio, this is the road to the airport. Why are we going to the airport?'

He kept driving, his hands steady on the wheel. 'Because I want to.'

'You want to eat plastic sandwiches in an airport?'

'You used to live on plastic sandwiches before you met me,' he reminded her in an amused voice, and she laughed.

'Maybe I did. But you've given me a taste for pasta. Gio, what is going on?' They'd arrived at the small airport and everything seemed to be happening around her.

Before she could catch her breath and form any more questions, she was standing on the runway, at the foot of a set of steps that led into the body of an aircraft.

'Go on. We don't want to miss our slot.' Gio walked up behind her, carrying two cases and she stared at them.

'What are those?'

'Our luggage.'

'I don't have any luggage. I was just coming out for a sandwich.' She brushed the hair out of her eyes, frustrated by the lack of answers she was receiving to her questions. 'Gio, what is going on?'

'I'm taking you to my favourite place to eat.'

'That's this evening. It's only one o'clock in the afternoon.' She watched as a man appeared behind them and took the cases onto the plane. 'Who's he? What's he doing with those?'

'He's putting them on the plane.' Gio took her arm. 'We're leaving at one o'clock because it takes a long time to get there, and we're going by plane because it's the best way to reach Sicily.'

'Sicily?' Her voice skidded and squeaked. 'You're taking me to *Sicily?*'

'You'll love it.'

Had he gone totally mad? 'I'm sure I'll love it and maybe I'll go there one day, but not on a Thursday afternoon when I have a well-woman clinic and a late surgery!' She looked over her shoulder, ready to make a dash back to the car, but he closed a hand over her arm and urged her onto the steps.

'Forget work, *tesoro.* It's all taken care of. David and Trisha are taking over for five days.'

'David?' With him so close behind her, she was forced to climb two more steps. 'What's he got to do with this? He's in London.'

'Not any more. He's currently back in your surgery, preparing for your well-woman clinic.' He brushed her hair away from her face and dropped a gentle kiss on her mouth. 'When did you last have a holiday, Alice?'

'I haven't felt the need for a holiday. I like my life.' She took another step upwards, her expression exasperated. 'Or, rather, I liked my life the way it was before everyone started interfering!'

He urged her up another step. 'I'll do you a deal— if, after this weekend, you want to go back to your old life, I'll let you. No arguments.'

'But I can't just—'

He nudged her forwards. 'Yes, you can.'

'You're kidnapping me in broad daylight!'

'That's right. I am.' His broad shoulders blocked her

exit and she made a frustrated sound in her throat and turned and stomped up the remaining steps.

This was totally ridiculous!

It was—

She stopped dead, her eyes widening as she saw the cabin. It was unlike any plane she'd ever seen before. Two soft creamy leather sofas faced each other across a richly carpeted aisle. A table covered in crisply laundered linen was laid for lunch, the silver cutlery glinting in the light.

Her mouth dropped.

'This isn't a plane. It's a living room.' Glancing over her shoulder, she realised that she'd been so distracted by the fact he was planning to take her away, she hadn't been paying attention. 'We didn't come through the airport the normal way.'

'This is a private plane.' He pushed her forward and nodded to the uniformed flight attendant who was smiling and waiting for them to board.

'Private plane?' Not knowing what else to do, she walked towards the sofas, feeling bemused and more than a little faint. 'Whose private plane?'

He sat down next to her. 'My brother, Marco, has made quite a success of his olive oil business.' Gio's tone was smooth as he leaned across to fasten her seat belt before placing another kiss on her cheek. 'It has certain compensations for the rest of his family. And now, *tesoro*, relax and prepare to be spoiled.'

She wished he'd stop touching her.

She couldn't think or concentrate when he touched her and she had a feeling that she was really, really going to need to concentrate.

CHAPTER TEN

THE moment the plane landed, Alice knew it was possible to fall in love. With a country, at least.

And as they drove away from the airport and along the coast, the heat of the sun warmed her skin and lifted her spirits. It was summer in Cornwall, of course, but somehow it didn't feel the same.

As she relaxed in her seat and watched the country fly past, all she knew was that that she'd never seen a sky more blue or a sea that looked more inviting. As they drove, the coast was a golden blur of orange and lemon orchards and she wanted to beg Gio to stop the car, just so that she could pick the fruit from the tree.

As if sensing the change in her, he reached across and rested a hand on her leg, his other hand steady on the wheel. 'It is beautiful, no?'

'Wonderful.' She turned to look at him. 'Where are we going?'

'Always you ask questions.' With a lazy smile in her direction, he returned his hand to the wheel. 'We are going to dinner, *tesoro*. Just as I promised we would.'

The warmth of the sun and the tantalising glimpses of breathtaking coastline and ancient historical sights distracted her from delving more deeply, and it was early evening when Gio pulled off the main road, drove down a dusty lane and into a large courtyard.

Alice was captivated. 'Is this where we're staying? It's beautiful. Is it a hotel?'

'It has been in my family for at least five generations,' Gio said, opening the boot and removing the cases. 'It's home.'

'Home?' The smile faded and she felt nerves flicker in the pit of her stomach. 'You're taking me to meet your parents.'

'Not just my parents, *tesoro*.' He slammed the boot shut and strolled over to her, sliding a hand into her hair and tilting her head. 'My whole family. Everyone lives in this area. We congregate here. We exchange news. We show interest in each other's lives. We offer support when it's needed and praise when it's deserved and quite often when it isn't. But most of all we offer unconditional love. It's what we do.'

'But I—'

'Hush.' He rested a finger on her lips to prevent her from speaking. 'You don't believe in love, Alice Anderson, because you've never seen it. But after this weekend you will no longer be able to use that excuse. Welcome to Sicily. Welcome to my home.'

She looked a little lost, he thought to himself, seated among his noisy, ebullient family. A little wary. As if she had no idea how to act surrounded by a large group of people who so clearly adored each other.

As his mother piled the table high with Sicilian delicacies, his father recounted the tale of his latest medical drama in his severely restricted English and Gio saw Alice smile. And respond.

She was shy, he noticed. Unsure how to behave in a large group. But they drew her into the conversation in the way that his family always welcomed any guest at their table. The language was a mix of Italian and English. English when they addressed her directly and could find the words, Italian when the levels of excitement bubbled over and they restarted to their native tongue with much hand waving and voice raising, which would have sent a lesser person running for cover. His grandmother spoke only a Sicilian dialect and his younger sister, Lucia, acted as interpreter, her dark eyes sparkling as she was given the opportunity to show off her English in public.

And gradually Alice started to relax. After eating virtually nothing, he saw her finally lift her fork. He intercepted his mother's look of approval and understanding.

And knew that he'd been right to bring her.

The buzz of conversation still ringing in her ears, Alice followed Gio out into the semi-darkness. 'Where are we going?'

'I don't actually live in the house any more.' He took her hand and led her towards a track that wound through a citrus orchard towards the sea. 'Years ago my brother and I built a small villa at the bottom of the orchard. The idea was to let it to tourists but then we decided we wanted to keep it. He's long since moved to something more extravagant but I keep this place as a bolthole. I love my family but even I need space from them.'

'I thought they were lovely.' She couldn't keep the envy out of her voice and suddenly she stopped walking and just stood and stared. Tiny lights illuminated the path that ran all the way to the beach. The air was warm and she could smell the fruit trees and hear the lap of the sea against the sand. 'This whole place is amazing. I just can't imagine it.'

'Can't imagine what?'

'Growing up here. With those people.' She took her hand away from his and reached out to pick a lemon from the nearest tree. It fell into her hand, complete with leaves and stalk, and she stared at it, fascinated. 'It's no wonder you believe in love, Dr Moretti. I think it would be possible to believe in just about anything if you lived here.'

He stepped towards her. Took her face in his hands. 'And do you believe in it, Alice? You met my family this evening. My parents have been together for almost forty years, my grandparents for sixty-two years. I believe that my great-grandparents were married for sixty-five years, although no one can be sure because no one can actually remember a time when they weren't together.' His thumb stroked her cheek. 'What did you see tonight, Alice? Was it convenience? Friendship? Any of those reasons you once gave me for people choosing to spend their lives together?'

Her heart was thumping in her chest and she shook her head slowly. 'No. It was love.' Her voice cracked as she said the words. 'I saw love.'

'Finally.' Gio closed his eyes briefly and murmured something in Italian. 'Let's go—I want to show you how I feel about you.'

* * *

It was tender and loving, slow and drawn out, with none of the fevered desperation of their previous encounters. Flesh slid against flesh, hard male against soft female, whispers and muttered words the only communication between them.

The bedroom of the villa opened directly onto the beach and she could hear the sounds of the sea, feel the night air as it flowed into the room and cooled them.

Long hours passed. Hours during which they feasted and savoured, each reluctant to allow the other to sleep.

And finally, when her body was so languid and sated that she couldn't imagine ever wanting to move again, he rolled onto his side and looked into her eyes.

'I love you, Alice.' His voice was quiet in the semi-darkness. 'I want you to be with me always. For ever. I want you to marry me, *tesoro.*'

'No, Gio.' The word made her shiver and she would have backed away but he held her tightly.

'Tonight you admitted that love exists.'

'For some other people maybe.' She whispered the words, almost as if she was afraid to speak them too loudly. 'But not for me.'

'Why not for you?'

'Because I don't—I can't—'

'Because when you were a child, your mother let you fall.' He lifted a hand and stroked the hair away from her face. 'She let you fall and now you don't trust anyone to be there to catch you. Isn't that right, Alice?'

'It isn't—'

'But you have to learn to trust. For the first time in your life you have to learn.' His mouth hovered a mere breath away from hers. 'You can fall, Alice. You can fall, *tesoro,* and I'll be standing here ready to catch you. Always. That's what love is. It's a promise.'

Tears filled her eyes. 'You make it sound so perfect and simple.'

'Because it is both perfect and simple.'

'No.' She shook her head and let the tears fall. 'That is what my mother thought. Every time she was with a man she had these same feelings and she thought they were love. But they turned out to be something entirely different. Something brittle and destructive. My father was the same. And I have their genes. I believe that *you* can love, but I don't believe the same of myself. I can't do it. I'm not capable of it.'

'You are still afraid.' He brushed the tears away with his thumb. 'You think that you are still that little girl on the climbing frame, but you're not. Over the past few weeks I've watched you and I've seen you learning to touch and be touched. I've seen you becoming comfortable with other people's emotions. All we need to do now is make you comfortable with your own.'

'It won't work, Gio. I'm sorry.'

Their bags were packed and Gio was up at the house having a final meeting with his brother about family business. She hovered in the courtyard, enjoying the peace and tranquillity of the setting.

After four days of lying on the beach and swimming in the pool, she should have felt relaxed and refreshed. Instead, she felt tense and miserable. And the last thing she wanted was to go home.

From the courtyard of the main house she stared down through the citrus orchard to the sea and then glanced behind her, her eyes on the summit of Mount Etna, which dominated the skyline.

'We will miss you when you've gone. You must come again soon, Alice.' Gio's mother walked up behind her and gave her a warm hug.

'Thank you for making me feel so welcome.' The stiffness inside her subsided and she hugged the older woman back, envying Gio his family.

'Anyone who has taught my Gio to smile again will always be welcome here.'

Alice pulled away slightly. 'He always smiles.'

'Not since the accident. He was frustrated. Sad. Grieving for the abilities that he'd lost. His ability to help all those poor little children. You have shown him that a new life is possible. That change can be good. You have given him a great deal. But that is what love is all about. Giving.'

Alice swallowed. 'I haven't—I don't—'

'You will come and see us again soon. You must promise me that.'

'Well, I…' she licked her lips, 'Gio will probably want to bring some other girl—'

His mother frowned. 'I doubt it.' Her voice was quiet. 'You are the first girl he has ever brought home, Alice.'

The first girl?

Alice stared at her and the other woman smiled.

'He has had girlfriends, yes, of course. He is an attractive, healthy young man so that is natural. But love…' She gave a fatalistic shrug. 'That only happens to a man once in a lifetime, and for my Giovanni it is now. Don't take too long to realise that you feel the same way, Alice. To lose something so precious would be nothing short of a tragedy.'

With that she turned and walked back across the courtyard into the house, leaving Alice staring after her.

Gio stood on the beach and stared out to sea, unable to drag himself away. Disappointment sat in his gut like a lead weight that he couldn't shift.

He'd relied on this place, *his home,* to provide the key he needed. To unlock that one remaining part of Alice that was still hidden away. But his plan had failed.

Maybe he'd just underestimated the depth of the damage that her parents had done to her.

Or maybe he was wrong to think that she loved him. Maybe she didn't love him at all.

'Gio?' Her voice sounded tentative, as if she wasn't sure of her welcome, and he turned with a smile. It cost him in terms of effort but he was determined that she shouldn't feel bad. None of this was her fault. None of it.

He glanced at his watch. 'You're right—we should be leaving. Are you ready?'

'No. No, I'm not, actually.' She stepped away from him, a slender figure clothed in a blue dress that dipped at the neck and floated past her knees. Her feet were bare and she was wearing a flower in her hair.

The transformation was complete, he thought to himself sadly. A few weeks ago her wardrobe had all been about work. Practical skirts and comfortable shoes. Neat tops with tailored jackets.

Now she looked relaxed and feminine. Like the exquisitely beautiful woman that she was.

'Well, you have five more minutes before we have to

leave.' He prompted her gently. 'If there are still things you need to fetch, you'd better fetch them fast.'

'There's nothing I need to fetch.' In four days on the beach her pale skin had taken on a soft golden tone and her blonde hair fell silky smooth to her shoulders. 'But there are things that I need to say.'

'Alice—'

'No, I really need to be allowed to speak.' She stood on tiptoe and covered his lips with her fingers, the way he'd done to her so many times. 'I didn't realise. I didn't realise that giving up surgery had meant so much to you. You hid that well.'

He tensed. 'I—'

'It's nice to know that other people hide things, too. That it isn't just me. It makes me realise that everyone has things inside them that they don't necessarily want to share.' She let her fingers drop from his mouth. 'It doesn't stop you from moving forward. It's nice to know that, even though you didn't smile for a while, you're smiling again now. And it's nice to know that I'm the only woman that you've ever brought home.'

'You've been speaking to my mother.'

'Yes.' She glanced down at her feet. Curled her toes into the sand. 'And I want it to stay that way. I want to be the first and last woman that you ever bring here. I should probably tell you that I'm seriously in love with your mother. And your sisters and brother, grandparents, uncles and aunts.'

'You are?' Hope flickered inside him, and the tiny flicker grew as she lifted her head and looked at him, her blue eyes clear and honest.

'You're right that I'm afraid. I'm afraid that everything that's in my past might get in the way of our future. I'm afraid that I might mess everything up.' She swallowed and took a deep breath, her hands clasped in front of her. 'I'm afraid of so many things. But love only happens once in a lifetime and it's taken me this long to find it so I can't let my fear stand in my way.' She held out her hand and lifted her chin. 'I'm ready to climb, Gio, if you promise that you'll be there to catch me. I'm ready to marry you, if you'll still have me.'

He took her hand, closed his eyes briefly and pulled her hard against him. 'I love you and I will always love you, even when you're ninety and you're still trying to talk to me about work when all I want to do is lie in the sun and look at my lemon trees.'

She looked up at him, eyes shining, and he felt his heart tumble. 'I have another confession to make—I haven't actually been thinking about work as much lately.'

'Is that so, Dr Anderson?' His expression was suddenly serious. 'And that's something that we haven't even discussed. What we do about work. Where we are going to live.' Did she want to stay in Cornwall? Was she thinking of moving to Italy?

She shrugged her shoulders. 'It doesn't matter.'

He couldn't hide his surprise. 'Well, I—'

'What matters is us,' she said quietly, her hand still in his. 'You've shown me that. I love you, Gio, and I always will. I believe in love now. A love that can last. This place makes me believe that. You make me believe it.'

For the first time in his adult life words wouldn't come, so he bent his head and kissed her.

Exclusively His

Back in his bed—and he's better than ever!

Whether you shared his bed for one night—
or five years—certain men are impossible to forget!
He might be your ex, but when you're back in his bed,
the passion is not just hot, it's scorching!

Things get tricky for sensible Veronica when
she unexpectedly meets Lucien again after one
night in Paris. And now he's determined to
seduce her back into his bed....

PUBLIC SCANDAL, PRIVATE MISTRESS
by *Susan Napier*
#2777

Available in November.

*Look out for more Exclusively His novels
in Harlequin Presents in 2009!*

www.eHarlequin.com   HP12777

MEDITERRANEAN PRINCES

Playboy princes, island brides—
bedded and wedded by royal command!

Roman and Nico Magnati—
Mediterranean princes with undisputed
playboy reputations!

These powerfully commanding princes expect
their every command to be instantly obeyed—and
they're not afraid to use their well-practiced seduction
to get what they want, when they want it....

THE MEDITERRANEAN
PRINCE'S CAPTIVE
VIRGIN
by Robyn Donald
#2776

Available in November.

REQUEST YOUR FREE BOOKS!

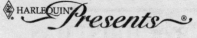

2 FREE NOVELS PLUS 2 FREE GIFTS!

YES! Please send me 2 FREE Harlequin Presents® novels and my 2 FREE gifts (gifts are worth about $10). After receiving them, if I don't wish to receive any more books, I can return the shipping statement marked "cancel". If I don't cancel, I will receive 6 brand-new novels every month and be billed just $4.05 per book in the U.S. or $4.74 per book in Canada, plus 25¢ shipping and handling per book and applicable taxes, if any*. That's a savings of close to 15% off the cover price! I understand that accepting the 2 free books and gifts places me under no obligation to buy anything. I can always return a shipment and cancel at any time. Even if I never buy another book, the two free books and gifts are mine to keep forever.

106 HDN ERRW 306 HDN ERRL

Name _____ (PLEASE PRINT) _____

Address _____ Apt. # _____

City _____ State/Prov. _____ Zip/Postal Code _____

Signature (if under 18, a parent or guardian must sign)

Mail to the **Harlequin Reader Service:**
IN U.S.A.: P.O. Box 1867, Buffalo, NY 14240-1867
IN CANADA: P.O. Box 609, Fort Erie, Ontario L2A 5X3

Not valid to current subscribers of Harlequin Presents books.

Want to try two free books from another line?
Call 1-800-873-8635 or visit www.morefreebooks.com.

* Terms and prices subject to change without notice. N.Y. residents add applicable sales tax. Canadian residents will be charged applicable provincial taxes and GST. Offer not valid in Quebec. This offer is limited to one order per household. All orders subject to approval. Credit or debit balances in a customer's account(s) may be offset by any other outstanding balance owed by or to the customer. Please allow 4 to 6 weeks for delivery. Offer available while quantities last.

Your Privacy: Harlequin Books is committed to protecting your privacy. Our Privacy Policy is available online at www.eHarlequin.com or upon request from the Reader Service. From time to time we make our lists of customers available to reputable third parties who may have a product or service of interest to you. If you would prefer we not share your name and address, please check here. ☐

HP08R

MARRIED BY CHRISTMAS

For better or worse—she'll be his by Christmas!

As the festive season approaches, these darkly handsome Mediterranean men are looking forward to unwrapping their brand-new brides.... Whether they're living luxuriously in London or flying by private jet to their glamorous European villas, these arrogant, commanding tycoons need a wife...and they'll have one— by Christmas!

HIRED: THE ITALIAN'S CONVENIENT MISTRESS
by CAROL MARINELLI (Book #29)

THE SPANISH BILLIONAIRE'S CHRISTMAS BRIDE
by MAGGIE COX (Book #30)

CLAIMED FOR THE ITALIAN'S REVENGE
by NATALIE RIVERS (Book #31)

THE PRINCE'S ARRANGED BRIDE
by SUSAN STEPHENS (Book #32)

Happy holidays from Harlequin Presents!

Available in November.

MARRIED BY CHRISTMAS

Playboy billionaire Elijah Vanaldi has discovered
he is guardian to his small orphaned nephew.
But his reputation makes some people question
his ability to be a father. He knows he must
fight to protect the child, and he'll do anything
it takes. Ainslie Farrell is jobless, homeless and
desperate—and when Elijah offers her a position
in his household she simply can't refuse....

Available in November

HIRED: THE ITALIAN'S CONVENIENT MISTRESS
by
CAROL MARINELLI
Book #29